DAPHNE

DAPHNE

DAPHNE

Being the Fourth Volume
of the Six Sisters

M.C. Beaton

WINDSOR
PARAGON

First published 1984
by Macdonald & Co (Publishers) Ltd
This Large Print edition published 2013
by AudioGO Ltd
by arrangement with
Constable & Robinson Ltd

Hardcover   ISBN: 978 1 4713 3380 4
Softcover   ISBN: 978 1 4713 3381 1

British Library Cataloguing in Publication Data available

Printed and bound in Great Britain by
MPG Books Group Limited

*To Andrew Porada, with love,
in memory of the Wall Street days.*

▉▉▉▉▉▉▉▉▉▉▉▉▉▉▉▉	
▉▉▉▉▉▉▉	
AudioGO	21.06.13
	£19.99
LP	

MISS BAILEY'S GHOST

A Captain bold, in Halifax, who dwelt in
    country quarters,
Seduced a maid who hang'd herself, one
    morning, in her garters,
His wicked conscience smited him, he lost his
    stomach daily,
He took to drinking ratafee, and thought upon
    Miss Bailey.
    Oh, Miss Bailey! unfortunate Miss Bailey.

One night betimes he went to rest, for he had
    caught a fever,
Says he, 'I am a handsome man, but I'm a gay
    deceiver;'
His candle just at twelve o'clock began to burn
    quite palely,
A ghost stepp'd up to his bed side, and said,
    'Behold Miss Bailey.'
    Oh, Miss Bailey! unfortunate Miss Bailey.

'Avaunt, Miss Bailey,' then he cried, 'your face
    looks white and mealy,'
'Dear Captain Smith,' the ghost replied,
    'you've used me ungenteelly;
The Crowner's Quest goes hard with me,
    because I've acted frailly,
And parson Biggs won't bury me, though I am
    dead Miss Bailey.'
    Oh, Miss Bailey! unfortunate Miss Bailey.

'Dear Corpse,' said he, 'since you and I
accounts must once for all close,
I've really got a one pound note in my
regimental small clothes;
'Twill bribe the sexton for your grave,'—The
ghost then vanished gaily,
Crying, 'Bless you, wicked Captain Smith,
remember poor Miss Bailey.'
Oh, Miss Bailey! unfortunate Miss Bailey.

Anon.

CHAPTER ONE

Lady Godolphin was suffering from a bad conscience. The comfortable travelling carriage bearing herself and young Daphne Armitage bowled smoothly along the summer roads of Berham county.

Daphne had been staying in London with her sister, Annabelle. Although she had just turned eighteen no plans had yet been made to bring her out, her father, the Reverend Charles Armitage, being in funds and therefore, for once, content to let his latest marriageable daughter age slightly before rushing her off to the altar.

But Daphne had met and fallen in love with a very beautiful young man at one of Lady Godolphin's parties and an engagement seemed in the offing. The man of her choice was Cyril Archer, famed in London society for his youth, beauty, and total lack of brain.

Lady Godolphin now felt uneasily she should have thrown a spoke in that particular wheel.

The elder Armitage girls had all married *men*, handsome, dashing, virile *men*, not empty-headed preening coxcombs. Minerva was comfortably wed to Lord Sylvester Comfrey, Annabelle to the Marquess of Brabington and Deirdre to Lord Harry Desire.

It was not as if Daphne had much in her cockloft either, reflected Lady Godolphin sourly. It was just that the vicar would not, she was sure, look on Daphne's choice with any warmth. Furthermore, Mr Archer was comfortably off, but hardly rich.

1

And Charles Armitage would no doubt blame her, Lady Godolphin, for having been instrumental in introducing Daphne to Mr Archer.

Lady Godolphin was a distant relative of the Armitages and had been much involved with the three elder girls' marriages. She was fond of all the Armitage girls, but could not help feeling Daphne had turned out something of a disappointment.

She had no *character*.

From being a mischievous hoyden she had turned into a dazzling beauty, utterly wrapped up in her own appearance.

A sudden ray of hope shone in Lady Godolphin's brain.

'Does young Archer hunt?' she asked.

Daphne was studying her own reflection in a steel mirror which she had drawn out of her reticule.

'Oh, no,' she said vaguely. 'He detests blood sports.'

'Lor!' said Lady Godolphin gloomily. 'Well, men are all a lot of follicles, anyways. I've given them up myself. I started at Lent and kept on goin'.'

'Yes?' said Daphne, adjusting a curl.

'And paint too.'

'I had noticed,' said Daphne with rare animation. Privately she thought Lady Godolphin looked a great deal younger without her customary mask of *blanc* and rouge.

Lady Godolphin looked like a well-scrubbed bulldog. Her heavy face was creased with worry and her mouth turned down at the corners.

'Are you not happy that I have found a suitable young man?' asked Daphne at last, putting away

2

the mirror.

'Well, I am, and I amn't. Fact is, he's a bore. That's what bothers me.'

'He has delicate and sweet manners and he loves me,' said Daphne with unwonted severity.

'Oh, ah. I just don't know what Charles is going to say.'

'Father? Oh, father never notices me.'

'I wouldn't say that. He always said you were the beauty o' the bunch.'

'I know *that*,' said Daphne with seemingly awful vanity.

Lady Godolphin leaned forward and jerked down the glass. The scent of wild thyme and marjoram wafted into the carriage on the hot summer air. Clouds of thistledown drifted and clung and drifted again over the deep green meadows by the river. The hedgerows were a riot of colour with purple and yellow vetch, yellow-headed wild parsnip and white clover. A flock of woodpigeons squabbled noisily over the still-orange rowan berries and brightly coloured butterflies performed their erratic dance in the sleepy air.

Lady Godolphin's eyes began to close. She was worrying over nothing. She wasn't a terribly *close* relative of the Armitages and she had already done more than enough for the other girls. Daphne was as empty and silly as Mr Archer. But Lady Godolphin sleepily remembered Daphne when she and Diana used to get up to all sorts of mad capers; a Daphne animated with wild, blown hair, flushed face, and no care for her clothes whatsoever.

Soon her mouth fell open and she began to snore.

Daphne studied her sleeping face for a few

moments. Then that elegant young lady stretched her arms above her head and yawned, gave her ribs a good scratch, and popped her feet on the seat opposite as she slouched back comfortably.

Without a spectator, Daphne's beauty ceased, as far as she was concerned, to exist. For her, beauty was an armour which you donned before facing the gaze of even your nearest and dearest. Beauty, Daphne had found, excused everything from lack of dowry to lack of intelligence. So long as she looked beautiful and smiled prettily, then she did not need to exert herself in any way. Beauty meant you were loved by one and all.

Only look how poor little Diana got nothing but the rough edge of her father's tongue because she *would* hang around the stables and kennels, wishing out loud she could have been born a boy.

The sun sank lower in the sky and flocks of rooks sailed towards the woods. The sky paled to a greenish colour, then violet, then purple. One by one, the lights went on in farm cottages, flickering smears of yellow against the heavy glass.

Houses began to appear on either side of the road as they neared the county town of Hopeminster. They rattled through the quiet cobbled streets and out onto the road which led to the village of Hopeworth.

Daphne was at peace with the world. No longer would she have to dread a Season, or that her father should suddenly find himself out of pocket and hasten to marry her off to the first man with money. Cyril Archer suited her perfectly. He was a beautiful counterpart to herself. He never said anything startling or clever; in fact he rarely said anything at all. He had kissed her before she left, a

4

chaste kiss on the brow.

But he did seem to sail like some beautiful angel fish through that mysterious world of the *ton*, that world of shibboleths and taboos. It was as if he had been born in the middle of Almack's and cut his teeth at the opera. By instinct rather than intelligence did he manage to be socially correct at all times, weaving his way deftly through the saloons of the west end of London like an elegant dancer in an elaborate quadrille.

'Or Theseus in the Labyrinth,' said Daphne unconsciously speaking aloud.

'What!' said Lady Godolphin.

'I didn't know you were awake,' said Daphne, straightening her spine, and placing her feet neatly, side by side, on the carriage floor. 'I said like Theseus in the Labyrinth. In Crete, you know.'

'Your grammar is awful,' said Lady Godolphin, shaking her head so vigorously that her turban fell over one eye. '*Thoses* in the laburnum, not Theses.'

The carriage suddenly lumbered to a halt.

'We can't be there already!' exclaimed Lady Godolphin. She stuck her head out of the window. 'What's to do?'

'Don't know, my lady,' came the coachman's voice, 'but we'd better get out the pistols. Lights bobbing on the road ahead. Hope they ain't highwaymen.'

'Not near Hopeworth,' said Daphne calmly. 'Papa would not allow it.'

A faint halloo echoed from down the road. 'Someone's walking towards the carriage, my lady,' came the coachman's voice.

Lady Godolphin put a hand in the pocket in the door of the coach and pulled out a serviceable

5

horse pistol.

'Don't be affeart, Daphne,' said Lady Godolphin, her jowls quivering. 'They shan't touch us. Oh, for Heaven's sake, wench! Stop fiddling with your bonnet.'

'I am persuaded it is something to do with Papa, or something that he knows of,' said Daphne with what Lady Godolphin considered an air of absolute bovine stupidity.

There was the sound of voices and a head appeared at the carriage window. Lady Godolphin raised the pistol in both hands, closed her eyes tightly, and fired. Daphne knocked her arm up and the ball buried itself in the roof of the coach.

The window of the carriage was down. Daphne put her head out and said gently to the figure lying flat on the ground, 'It is all right, Papa. Lady Godolphin took you for a highwayman.'

The vicar of St Charles and St Jude struggled to his feet and crammed his shovel hat, which had fallen off, onto his head again. His squat figure trembled with outrage.

'Be damned to you, ma'am,' he gasped. 'You nearly sent me to my Maker!'

'It's your fault,' said Lady Godolphin, as much shaken as the outraged vicar. 'If you would behave more like a parson than a . . . than a . . *thing*. Parsons is in their churches, not cavortin' around the middle of the road.'

'And you should've told me you were coming,' said the vicar. 'Carriage can't get through. You and Daphne will need to get down and walk. There's a gurt hole in the middle o' the road.'

'I sent a letter,' said Lady Godolphin.

'Oh, is that what it was?' said the vicar, looking

6

uncomfortable. 'Never opened it. Thought it would be full o' female chit-chat. Get down. Get down. Tell you about it on the road home.'

Wheezing and puffing, Lady Godolphin climbed down from the carriage, followed by Daphne.

John Summer'll come over the fields with the hand cart and take your trunks to the vicarage,' said the Reverend Charles in an abstracted way. He seemed to have recovered quickly although he was plainly worried about something. 'The coach and your servants can return to Hopeminster, ma'am,' went on the vicar. 'Come along. Step lightly. No time to waste.'

Puffing and demanding explanations, Lady Godolphin with Daphne in tow followed him down the road. Both women were, however, struck speechless by the sight that met their eyes.

A group of labourers from the village had broken up a deep channel right across the road. The resultant pit was filled with ditchwater and was being carefully covered with turf and dust.

'Hunting has driven you mad,' exclaimed Lady Godolphin. 'I thought you considered it Sacker-lodges to kill reynard by any other means than hunting the beast down with an expensive pack o' hounds. But now it seems as if you're trying to trap the animal. Well, let me tell you, foxes don't go jauntering down the Hopeworth road. They keeps to the fields. They . . .

'It ain't for the fox,' said the vicar heavily. 'It's for the bishop.'

'Lud!'

'He's coming early in the morning for to pay me a visit. He's going to ask me to give up my pack.'

'Not Dr Jameson,' said Lady Godolphin,

remembering that the bishop usually kept as well away from Hopeworth parish as possible.

'New bishop,' said the vicar tersely. 'Dr Philpotts. Sent word. Said huntin' wasn't fit for a member o' the church.'

'But the poor man will break his neck!'

'Not he,' said the vicar. 'But it should make him think twice about goin' further.'

'It is a very *deep* pit, Papa,' ventured Daphne.

'Don't criticize things you know nothing about,' said the vicar. 'Not the sort of thing for girls or ladies to get exercised about.'

Lady Godolphin realized she was too tired to argue. Her feet ached. She never really had understood country life anyway. No need to refine too much on it and exhaust oneself by making a scene about nothing For all she knew, country vicars regularly dug pits for their bishops.

'How did you fare in London?' asked the vicar, turning his attention to Daphne.

Lady Godolphin squeezed Daphne's arm as a signal that it was not a very opportune time to talk about Mr Archer.

'Very well, Papa,' said Daphne demurely. 'I was much admired.'

'Not right for you to say so,' grunted the vicar. 'How goes Annabelle?'

'Well . . I think,' said Daphne cautiously.

'So she should be. Finally got that son she craved.'

'Yes,' said Daphne, shaking her head slightly as if to shake loose uncomfortable images of Annabelle absorbed in the welfare of her squat, ugly baby boy while her husband did not seem able to look at the child.

'And Minerva? And Deirdre?'

'Gone to Brighton, as you know, with the Fashionables, Papa. London was very thin of company. How are the little girls?' asked Daphne, meaning seventeen-year-old Diana and sixteen-year-old Frederica, her two younger sisters.

'Diana needs some teaching as to how to go on. She's run wild. And Frederica's sadly off in looks. Need to do something to bring them up to the mark.'

'That's all he ever thinks when he thinks of us girls,' thought Daphne dismally. 'We must be beautiful—the beautiful Armitage girls. Our value on the Marriage Mart must be kept high.'

Bravely, in order to turn her father's thoughts from her younger sisters, Daphne plunged in with, 'I am about to become affianced, Papa.'

The vicar stopped stock still and glared at Lady Godolphin's fast retreating back.

'Who to?'

'Cyril Archer.'

'*Mr* Cyril Archer.'

'Yes, Papa. But he is a fine young man. The Somerset Archers, you know.'

'No, I don't. What has her ladyship to say to this? What was Annabelle thinking of not to inform me?'

'Well, Annabelle is much concerned with baby Charles and . . . and . . . I met Mr Archer at Lady Godolphin's.'

The vicar breathed through his nose. 'I'll get to the bottom of this, miss.' He eyed her narrowly. A full moon had risen, outlining Daphne's trim figure, mondaine dress and beautiful face. 'You could marry a duke,' said the vicar sourly.

'I am sure you would put my happiness

before all worldly concerns,' said Daphne with a primness worthy of her sister Minerva at her most sanctimonious.

'We'll see,' said the vicar truculently. He was about to pursue the subject when his sharp little eyes spied the figure of Squire Radford on the other side of the village pond.

He did not want the squire to find out about the trap he had set for the bishop and so he hustled Daphne along the road as fast as he could.

When they reached the iron gates of the vicarage the vicar hissed, 'Mrs Armitage don't know nothing about the bishop, nor the girls either, so don't you go sayin' anything. Lor'! I forgot to warn Lady Godolphin.' He charged off into the house, leaving Daphne to follow.

Mrs Armitage was not belowstairs to welcome Daphne home. That good lady had overdosed herself with patent medicine which had brought on one of her Spasms. Frederica was already in bed but Diana was waiting in the small parlour with wine, and cakes.

'I heard of your arrival,' said Diana. 'Jem from the village came running up about ten minutes ago.'

Daphne sat down sedately, spine straight as a ramrod, and neatly removed her gloves. Then she unpinned her bonnet and laid it carefully on a chair. Diana, who was wearing a much-stained riding dress, looked at her elder sister with contempt. 'Still the same fashion plate, Daphne. I had hoped London might have *humanized* you. Oh, never mind. Tell me about Annabelle and the new baby.'

Daphne began to talk in her soft voice. Everything was well with Annabelle. The baby

10

was lusty and healthy and had a fine voice. Behind Daphne's calm brow flowed two streams of worry. What if the bishop broke his neck? Why had things at Annabelle's been so uncomfortable and *edgy?*

Diana listened, surveying Daphne curiously and wondering if anything ever troubled her apart from a stray curl. Daphne's midnight hair was arranged tastefully in artistic curls. She was a fashionable beauty, reflected Diana without even a tinge of jealousy. Straight little nose, large liquid eyes, and a small, beautifully shaped mouth.

'And then we met Father out on the Hopeworth road,' Daphne ended up.

'Really? What on earth was Father doing? And you and Lady Godolphin arrived on foot. A Lady Godolphin sans paints and sans cicisbeo, no less.'

'She gave both up for Lent and has become accustomed to doing without either,' said Daphne. 'I must retire,' she added hurriedly, wishing to avoid lying about what Father had been doing on the Hopeworth road.

Diana followed her upstairs. 'I wish you would speak on my behalf to Papa,' she said.

Daphne turned, her hand on the bannister. 'Why? Are you in love? Is there some gentleman?'

'Pooh. Of course not. I wish to ride to hounds next time Papa goes hunting.'

'But Diana,' pleaded Daphne, her large eyes even larger in amazement. 'You cannot! Only very coarse ladies go hunting.'

'Stuff! I can ride better than Papa, I will have you know. But he will not listen to me. *Please* Daphne?'

Daphne slowly began to walk up the stairs. 'I have not much influence with Papa,' she said over her shoulder. 'Minerva . . .'

11

'*Minerva!* Don't talk fustian. Minerva would read me a sermon!'

'But it is not very ladylike,' persisted Daphne, walking into her bedroom. 'You will soon wish to marry and you would not want the gentleman to have a disgust of you.'

'I don't *want* to get married!' said Diana fiercely. 'I want to hunt and shoot and fish. 'Member what fun we used to have before you became so hoity-toity, Daphne. But you love clothes and dressing up and being bored by a lot of social chit-chat. *Please* Daphne.'

Daphne sat down on the bed and looked at Diana, her calm gaze revealing none of the busy thoughts underneath. Diana's hair was worn behind her ears in a severe knot. Her mouth was rather large for beauty but her skin was flawless and her large, sparkling, black eyes gave her face a gypsy look which was oddly attractive.

All at once Daphne envied Diana who had confidence in herself and knew what she wanted. She, Daphne, had once run wild about the woods and fields. But that was before she had discovered her own beauty could save her such a great deal of pain. People did not say cutting or hurtful things if you were beautiful. They did not seem to expect you to say very much either. 'I will try, Diana,' she said slowly. 'But give me a little time.'

Diana gave her a hug, nearly knocking her back across the bed.

After she had left, Daphne carefully began to prepare for bed. John Summer had deposited her trunks, and the maid, Betty, had already hung her dresses and mantles away. Her heavy iron cosmetic box had been placed on the toilet table. Daphne

12

would allow no one to unpack these precious articles but herself. Carefully she began to take out each item and arrange them in order on the table. There were four different types of rouge—vegetable, serviette (to be applied with a cloth), Liquid Bloom of Roses, and cosmetic wool (treated with red dye).

Then there was a large bottle of Vento's Italian Water; a box of face powder called Powder Pearl of India, and a large swansdown puff. There was cold cream, beautifying cream, Pomade de Nerole and Pomade de Graffa.

Daphne used very little of these cosmetics, but she collected them as a magpie collects glittering objects. After she had admired her collection, she removed the little rouge she had on her cheeks with cleansing cream. It was when she was twisting this way and that to try to unfasten the tapes at the back of her dress that she realized the maid, Betty, had not put in an appearance to help her for bed. Betty had been elevated to lady's maid and a new parlourmaid called Sarah graced the vicarage. Although Betty had often acted as lady's maid when the sisters went to London on visits, she had always had to resume her lower position when she returned to the vicarage. But her promotion had been the result of some only half-heard row that John Summer had had with the vicar. Betty never seemed happy these days, thought Daphne, and she had never married John either, although at one point shortly after Deirdre's wedding, they had received Mr Armitage's blessing.

The vicar was still rather mean when it came to the number of servants he employed. John Summer still acted as groom, coachman, kennel master, and

13

whipper-in. The knife boy was still the pot boy as well as the page, and Sarah, the new housemaid, doubled as parlourmaid when the occasion demanded. There was a cook-housekeeper, Mrs Hammer, who held sway in the kitchen, and an odd-man who donned butler's livery if the guests were very grand.

Betty had been in London when the eldest Armitage girl, Minerva, had made her come-out, and had subsequently returned with the next in line, Annabelle, and had been there when Deirdre had been wed. She had been happy and cheerful, cheeky and frightened by turns, and after Deirdre's wedding had shown signs of settling down to marry John Summer and live happily ever after.

Then she had become ill and had been ill for quite some time—so ill that Mr Armitage had sent her away to the seaside in the hope that the fresh air of the ocean would cure her.

The visit seemed to have effected a physical cure but had done nothing to improve the maid's spirits. Betty had become surly and sad and no longer begged the girls' old dresses or tied pretty ribbons in her black curls.

'I must not worry so much,' thought Daphne, as she at last pulled a printed cotton nightgown over her head and slipped between the sheets. 'I will have wrinkles if I worry overmuch.

'But I *do* hope the bishop does not come!' Daphne, despite her worries, fell asleep very quickly. She had not thought of Mr Archer once.

*   *   *

The sun shone bravely in Daphne's bedroom

14

window at six in the morning. She awoke and blinked and then buried her face in the pillow and tried to go back to sleep. But a picture of the Bishop of Berham breaking his neck rose before her eyes to be followed by a picture of her father being hanged in front of Newgate Prison.

Daphne wondered whether to wake Diana and enlist her help. But Diana was her younger sister and must be shielded from harm.

It would not be so very bad, thought Daphne, if she dressed and walked to where the pit was so carefully concealed in the road and shouted a warning should the bishop's carriage appear.

Papa had said something about the bishop arriving early in the morning.

When Daphne let herself quietly out of the house a half-hour later, she did not look like the usual fashion plate she presented to the world. Her hair was brushed back behind her ears and confined at the nape of her neck with a pink ribbon. She wore serviceable boots under a drab gown of brown cotton.

The summer morning was sweet and still. Birds chirped sleepily in the hedgerows. A hazy mist was rising from the fields like a gauze curtain at the pantomime before the transformation scene. A few threads of smoke climbed from cottage chimneys into the lazy air. Daphne hurried along the edge of the village pond and along past the tall gates of The Hall where her uncle, Sir Edwin Armitage, lived with his chilly wife and two plain daughters. The road wound over the River Blyne. The river gurgled and chuckled over smooth round stones and between tall banks of rushes, the only busy thing in that early morning's peace.

15

On past the blind shuttered windows of Lady Wentwater's mansion went Daphne. Lady Wentwater had not been in residence for over two years and her nephew Guy who had once been a slave-trader was rumoured to have gone to America. Rumour also had it that Sir Edwin's daughter, Emily, was still waiting for his return.

Daphne came out of the shade of the trees which surrounded Lady Wentwater's mansion and looked down the long ribbon of road which led towards the crossroads.

Her heart seemed to stop.

A light carriage was upended in the vicar's pit and a still figure was lying beside the road. The horses had climbed free and were standing nearby.

Daphne picked up her skirts and ran as fast as she could towards the prone figure. Once again, in her mind's eye, she could see her father dancing on the end of a rope.

The figure resolved itself into that of a man, a large man. He was bespattered with mud and water from head to foot. His face was covered in mud.

Daphne knelt down beside him and gently took his head on her lap. 'Don't be dead,' she whispered. 'Please say something.'

A large tear rolled down Daphne's nose and plopped onto the mud-covered face on her lap.

'My lord bishop,' said Daphne, praying aloud. 'It was a most wicked thing to do. Only say that you are alive so that you may forgive us.'

The man's eyes opened suddenly and he stared straight up into Daphne's face.

'Thank God!' sobbed Daphne, taking out a dainty, scented handkerchief and trying to scrub some of the mud from his face. The man struggled

16

to sit up and Daphne knelt back on her heels and stared at him anxiously.

Her dusky curls had escaped from their ribbon and were tumbling about her face. Her enormous eyes were dark and beseeching.

'Please give me your blessing,' she said.

'Certainly,' said the man in a dazed way. He studied her face for a few moments and then began to smile, his teeth very white against the smeared mud on his face.

He leaned forward and neatly clipped Daphne about the waist, and, before she could even begin to think what he meant to do, he had pulled her into his arms and ruthlessly kissed her. Daphne struggled, filled with fear; fear of the strange heat flooding her body, of the masculine strength of his arms, of the faint bristle of his chin against her face.

When he released her, she jumped to her feet, scrubbing her mouth with the sleeve of her dress.

He staggered unsteadily to his feet and gazed down at her.

Daphne took a deep breath. 'How dare . . .'

But shock and outrage stifled the rest of the exclamation. She received a smart slap across her bottom.

'Run along,' said the muddy gentleman, 'and get some help.'

Daphne opened and shut her mouth, anger robbing her momentarily of speech.

At last she found her voice. 'You, my lord bishop, are an insult to the cloth.'

'Inbreeding,' murmured the gentleman. 'No,' he said in a kind voice. 'I am not a bishop. Bishops are a very rare breed. You must not keep thinking every gentleman you meet is a bishop, you know.'

17

But you *must* be the bishop!' wailed Daphne. 'My father, the vicar, dug this pit especially to trap him!'

The tall gentleman looked down at her, his yellowish eyes filled with pity. 'There, there, my child,' he said. 'I shall manage for myself.'

He began to walk off down the road in the direction of Hopeworth. 'A tragedy,' he thought. 'Such a beautiful girl. She should not be allowed to wander about the countryside without some sort of keeper.'

A patter of light steps behind him made him turn round. 'Oh, sir,' gasped Daphne. 'Who are you?'

'My name is Garfield, Simon Garfield at your service.'

'Well, Mr Garfield, you must listen. You see I would like to help you but the bishop may come along at any moment and I must warn him.'

'Very well, my child,' said Mr Garfield. 'You stay here and . . . er . . . warn the bishop.' His horses had broken their traces and miraculously plunged free of the ditch. He had tethered them to a tree and left them to graze in the long grass at the side of the road.

He strode off, leaving Daphne twisting her hands in agitation.

Mr Garfield quickly made his way towards Hopeworth. His head throbbed and the bright sunlight hurt his eyes. He silently cursed his friend, Edwin Apsley, whose idea it had been that he should call on a certain Mr Armitage and buy a couple of hounds. Mr Garfield had been staying with friends on the other side of Hopeminster. Edwin had been with him but had had to rush off to town to stop his latest inamorata from leaving his protection and had hurriedly begged Mr Garfield

18

to oblige him in the matter of the hounds.

'Who is this fellow Armitage?' Mr Garfield had asked. 'How shall I find him?'

'Oh, just ask in Hopeworth village,' Edwin had said carelessly. 'Everyone knows him.'

Mr Garfield decided to find the residence of this Mr Armitage and demand help to raise his carriage from the hole in the road.

He puzzled momentarily over the plight of the poor mad Ophelia who had tried to come to his rescue. Her voice did not have a country burr, but her clothes were old and unfashionable. Poor demented thing. He would never have kissed her had he guessed she had several rooms to let in her pretty head.

He paused outside the gates of Lady Wentwater's mansion, but it was all too clearly deserted. He sighed and went on further, past the River Blyne. On the other side of the bridge, he saw the squat figure of a lady rapidly approaching. She was wearing a large muslin cap which imperfectly concealed a head of curl papers. She was in her undress: a negligee over an elaborate petticoat. Mr Garfield saw with a sinking heart that she appeared to be talking to herself. He decided to ignore her and go on and see if he could find some sane person in this mad world. He began to wonder if the blow to his head had affected his wits.

But as he, came abreast of the lady, she stopped him and said, 'I never was more shocked when Betty told me. Tigers and panters and leapinghards, yes, I says, but not bishops. Charles is gone out and no one else is awake and *she's* no use, her with her Spasms. It's her way of not facing up to things. Now if I had had Spasms every day of my life like *she* does, I would not be what I am today.'

Mr Garfield smiled in a placating sort of way and made to move on, but Lady Godolphin, for it was she, much flustered and worried having heard confirmation of the vicar's bishop trap from the maid, caught hold of his sleeve.

'Now you look like a gentleman,' said Lady Godolphin earnestly, peering up into Mr Garfield's face, 'albeit a muddy one. Would *you* do such a thing? For when he told me last night, I thought it was all a hum and he meant it for drainage. For when I thought about it, I thought I could not have heard aright. Not till Betty come in with the tea and says, "You'll never guess what master has been and done."

"Betty," says I, "he was maundering on about some such thing and made me walk from the carriage so that my feet still ache, and my Arthur's Eitis is so awful I feel like that boy with the foxes gnawing at his vitality, but mark my words, he was funning." "Not he," says Betty to me. "In dead earnest is t'master."'

Lady Godolphin paused for breath. Mr Garfield made a strange strangled sound in the back of his throat, pulled his arm free, and hastened off down the road.

He began to feel more ill and more dizzy than he had done when he had recovered consciousness.

There were some women at the well on the village green. In a faltering voice, he asked for Mr Armitage's direction, and following the pointing fingers, he stumbled on.

The vicar was in high alt. John Summer, who had been posted at the Hopeworth-Hopeminster crossroads for most of the night, had come back in

20

the very early hours to report that he had stopped a messenger from the bishop with a note to say his lordship was indisposed. Unfortunately, John Summer had ridden away from the crossroads a bare half-hour before Mr Garfield had made his appearance.

It was just beginning to strike Mr Armitage that he had not considered the possibility of any other traveller falling victim to his trap. He decided to make his way along to the pit and call the workmen to fill it in as soon as possible.

As he swung open the iron gates of the vicarage, he became aware of a tall, muddy figure, swaying slightly in the middle of the lane.

'See here,' said the vicar sternly, advancing on Mr Garfield. 'We all take a toss, but from the look of you, you have no one to blame but yourself. Never ride when you're dead drunk.'

'Oh God in Heaven,' said Mr Garfield weakly. 'I am in Bedlam.'

With that, he put his hand to his brow and collapsed unconscious at the feet of the startled vicar.

CHAPTER TWO

Lady Godolphin hurried on until she met Daphne who was sitting disconsolately beside the pit, the carriage wreck, and the two horses.

'Lud!' said Lady Godolphin, putting her hand to her heart. 'Never tell me the bishop's down in there.'

'No, Lady Godolphin,' said Daphne. 'But

21

someone did have an accident. A very tall man. He . . . he . . . was unconscious and I thought he was dead and . . and . . . I thought it was the bishop and asked for his blessing and he *kissed* me.'

'Now, now,' said Lady Godolphin, putting a fat arm around Daphne's shoulders. 'You're all overwritten. You must not mind. That must have been the gentleman I met a little way back. He was most odd and rude in his manner, and yet I have a feeling I have seen him somewhere before. What on earth made your father think of such a thing? I really thought he was joking. It's all that religion. It do turn a body's head so.'

'I do not think Papa suffers from an excess of religion,' said Daphne, mopping her streaming eyes with her now muddy handkerchief and getting streaks of mud on her face.

'Speak of the devil,' said Lady Godolphin cheerfully. 'Unless I am much mistaken, here comes your pa now.'

A squat figure on horseback was riding hell-for-leather towards them, sending up a cloud of white dust into the morning air.

The vicar reined in. 'John and some of the lads will be along in a minute to fill that in,' he said. 'Bishop's not coming. He's got the gout. "God hath chosen the foolish things of the world to confound the wise . . ." St Paul. Or in other words, his lordship might not have got the gout if he had not been so clutch-fisted with that port of his. Not that good port is a foolish thing; it's only foolish when you drink all of it yourself and offer your guests indifferent canary.'

'But Papa,' wailed Daphne. 'Someone did fall into your trap. A strange gentleman.'

22

'Oh, lor',' said the vicar dismally. 'I thought he was foxed. He's stretched out in the boys' room with cold cloths on his head. Best get the doctor to bleed him. I told Betty to leave him be to sleep it off. Kept opening his eyes, looking at me, saying "Oh, no," and collapsing again. I think he's touched in his upper works.'

'More like to have damaged his brain box in that silly trap of yours,' said Lady Godolphin. 'Hark'ee, Charles, you'd best hope he recovers or he'll have a mess of relatives along here sueing the life out of you.'

John Summer and a party of men came along the road. The vicar waited for them impatiently and then rapped out instructions to fill in the hole and 'make it look as if it weren't ever there'.

'For,' as he explained to Lady Godolphin and Daphne while they all walked off together, the vicar leading his horse, 'we can always deny that such a thing happened, and we can all stick together and swear that he took a toss when his carriage wheel hit a rock.'

On their return to the vicarage, Daphne and Lady Godolphin both announced their intention of retiring again to bed.

The vicar climbed the stairs and cautiously pushed open the door of the boys' room. The twins, Peregrine and James, were staying with their sister, Minerva, in Brighton. Their room had once been turned into a dressing room for the girls, but they had objected very strongly to this, saying that when they returned for the holidays, they did not want to bed down among a lot of fripperies and so it had been turned back to its former state.

The twins shared a large fourposter bed. In the

middle of it lay the still form of Mr Garfield.

He was lying on top of the covers. His face had been washed but he was still dressed in his muddy clothes. Despite the mud, the vicar's worldly eye recognized the genius of Weston's tailoring and his heart sank. The richer they came, the more likely they were to make trouble. As they had passed through the village he had called at the doctor's house, and the doctor had promised to step along.

John Summer was helping fill in the pit.

The vicar decided to summon the odd-man, Henry, and the pot boy, Billy, to help him strip the visitor and get him into a clean nightshirt before the doctor came.

This being achieved and the doctor closeted with the patient, the vicar, still worried about the possible importance of his unexpected guest, decided to rouse Daphne.

He stood looking down at the sleeping girl. Her hair was tumbled over the pillow and she looked, in repose, very much like the little girl who used to go rioting around the woods with Diana. For the first time, the vicar wondered uneasily what Daphne really thought about. He was very proud of her beauty although her calm, almost bovine expression exasperated him.

He realized he rather missed the old Daphne. He put a gentle hand on her shoulder and she came awake with a start, her eyes wide and clear, and then their expression suddenly shuttered as she focused on her father.

'I am monstrous sorry to wake you,' said the vicar. 'Did the gentleman tell you his name by any chance?'

'Oh, yes,' said Daphne sleepily. 'You see, it was

awful. I thought he was the bishop and asked for his blessing, and . . . and . . . he kissed me.'

'He did, did he?' said the vicar grimly 'I'll have a word with that gentleman as soon as he's on his feet. He'll soon learn that he can't play fast and loose with my daughters. That Guy Wentwater was enough!'

Daphne struggled up against the pillows.

'I remember his name, Papa. Garfield, he said it was. Mr Simon Garfield.'

The vicar's little shoe button eyes stretched to their widest and his mouth fell open.

Then a look of cunning mixed with one of satisfaction spread across his chubby face.

'Well, well,' he said, rubbing his hands. 'I wonder what brought him to Hopeworth.' He pinched Daphne's cheek. 'Clever puss,' he grinned. 'What's in a friendly kiss, hey?'

Daphne looked at her father in amazement. 'But, Papa, a moment before you were going to speak to Mr Garfield about his bold manners and . . .'

'Just a joke,' said the vicar. 'You're looking a bit bagged, Daphne. Not your usual pretty self. When you rise, wear that pretty blue thing of yours with the silk ribbons and get Betty to help you with your hair.'

Fully awake now and beginning to feel dimly alarmed, Daphne ventured, 'If you recall, Papa, I am about to become affianced to a most suitable young man. A Mr Archer.'

The vicar's brows snapped down. 'We'll see about that,' he said grimly. 'You're too young to choose a husband for yourself. Best leave that job to your father.'

'But Papa! You said we were in funds. You said

25

you no longer believed in arranged marriages. You said I could have any suitable man that took my fancy . . .'

'Don't recall,' said the vicar, strutting up and down the room. 'Let me see. Hope he ain't very ill. Now, remember Daphne. Not a word o' that there pit. As far as us Armitages are concerned, he imagined the whole thing. Well, well, well . . .'

The vicar bustled off leaving Daphne very confused and worried. This Mr Garfield must be very rich. Papa must already be viewing Mr Garfield in the light of a possible son-in-law. Daphne was therefore to forget about Mr Archer.

Now, in truth, Daphne had not entertained very warm feelings towards the beautiful Mr Archer. She enjoyed the admiration both of them excited, she felt at ease in his undemanding company. Mr Archer would never grab hold of her roughly and kiss her on the mouth. Mr Archer had never even shown any desire to kiss her on the mouth at all!

But at the thought that she had no free will as far as her father was concerned a slow ice-cold little stone of rebellion started growing somewhere in the pit of Daphne's stomach.

She, Daphne, had been a biddable, dutiful daughter. She had done her utmost to please her father by turning herself into a fashion plate—although, she admitted, it had also been to please herself.

She had felt that by armouring herself in beauty, she could escape her father's machinations and the occasional lash of his tongue. Now it seemed as if she were to be thrust willy-nilly into a marriage she did not want, before she had even had a Season or enjoyed any real balls or parties. And now Daphne wanted a Season, now that it seemed she wasn't going to have one.

Gradually Mr Archer grew in her mind into a passionate, romantic lover. She dwelt on his perfection, beginning to read wit into his every remembered vague utterance, and passion into the calm, blue, empty gaze of his eyes. No longer did Mr Archer appear as a marital refuge from the turmoil of this naughty world, but rather as a strong, noble, dream lover so soon to be lost.

Ah, but what did Mr Garfield think? Mr Garfield had obviously thought her, Daphne, insane. Therefore might it not be a good idea to foster that idea?

A wicked grin lit up Daphne's lovely features, which she immediately suppressed.

Excess of emotion caused wrinkles. She carefully arranged her face into its usual calm mask and decided to dress and go downstairs and start the first act of the comedy. Perhaps Mr Garfield would keep to his room. But if not, then she would be ready for him.

*   *   *

It is very hard for a gentleman to look formidable in a vicarage nightshirt but that is exactly what a shaved, washed and barbered Mr Garfield managed to do.

The vicar stood at the end of the bed, shuffling his feet, and looking like a guilty schoolboy. Mr Garfield had already despatched John Summer to the Chumleys on the other side of Hopeminster, with whom he had been staying, to fetch his travelling carriage, his servants and his clothes. As soon as they arrived, he pointed out in chilly accents, he would take his leave and would no doubt further his acquaintanceship with the reverend in court. The fact that he was dealing with a member of the clergy made Mr Garfield's anger the more severe.

Mr Garfield had not believed one word of the vicar's rambling explanation that he, Simon Garfield, had been momentarily touched in the upper-works and had imagined the whole thing.

A silence fell while the vicar wondered how to extricate himself from this coil. He wished he had sent for Squire Radford whose good sense had helped him out of so many scrapes in the past.

The pale light from a tall candle beside the bed shone on Mr Garfield's handsome, stone-like features. He was a very tall, very muscular man with peculiar yellowish eyes set under heavy lids. He had an autocratic high-bridged nose and a way of tilting his head back and staring awfully down it. His mouth was well-shaped, if a trifle thin. He had a strong chin and the powerful column of his throat rose above the lace at the neck of the vicar's best nightshirt.

'Furthermore, reverend,' he drawled, fixing the vicar with the yellow gaze of a hawk about to devour its prey, 'you can talk till doomsday about rocks and accidents but the fact remains that for some insane reason you dug a ditch across the road into which I fell, shattered my carriage, and nearly broke my neck.

'It is only by some miracle that my horses weren't badly hurt. I know you have offered to pay for the damage, but I feel you should be taken to court and

28

charged with your malicious folly. I came, as I told you, to buy a couple of hounds for a friend. I now would no longer deal with you that I would with a horse thief.'

'Be damned to you, sirrah,' said the much-plagued vicar suddenly losing his temper. 'Who are you to lie there in *my* bed, in *my* house, looked after by *my* servants, and preach at *me?* A fine gentleman you turned out to be. Trying to seduce my daughter.'

'I never met your . . .'

'Oh, yes you did. Yes you did!' said the little vicar, jumping up and down. 'You were mauling her and kissing her and all because she took you for the bishop.'

'Oh, *that* was your daughter. Well, more shame to you. That poor demented child should not be allowed out without a keeper.'

'What! My Daphne's as sane as I am.'

'Evidently,' said Mr Garfield acidly.

There was a rumbling of wheels outside. Mr Garfield climbed down from the high bed and crossed to the window and twitched aside the curtain. 'My servants and clothes at last,' he said. 'Be so good as to send my man up to me.'

'Send for him yourself, you . . . you . . . *coxcomb!*' howled the vicar.

'Very well.' Mr Garfield opened the window and called to his servants below.

The vicar marched from the room.

An hour later, Mr Garfield descended the narrow stairs of the vicarage. The house seemed very quiet and empty. He pushed open a door in the hall and discovered a cluttered study. He tried a door across the hall and found himself in the vicarage parlour. He was about to retreat when he realized there was a young lady present. And what a young lady! Midnight-black hair in rioting curls framed an exquisite face with wide-spaced dark eyes. He caught his breath and moved further into the room.

The gaze she turned on him was completely empty and he recognized with a pang of disappointment that he was looking at the poor Ophelia he had so mistakenly kissed by the roadside. He hoped she was not going to start mistaking him for a bishop again.

By the vicar's very guilt and denials, he felt he had come at the truth which was that the vicar had had a hole dug in the road to effect some repairs and then had gone off and carelessly left it. For which he heartily deserved to be punished. He was not like a vicar at all. But what were vicars supposed to be like? There were so many of these 'squarsons' around, so called because they were more squire than parson and cared more for hunting than they did for their parish duties.

Daphne lowered her eyes over the sewing in her lap, her heart beating hard. She had not realized Mr Garfield was so very imposing. He was impeccably dressed in a blue swallowtail coat with a high velvet collar. His biscuit-colour pantaloons were moulded to a pair of powerful thighs and his hessian boots shone like black glass.

A quizzing glass was dangling from his lapel. 'What is your name, my child?' he asked gently. 'Daphne Armitage,' answered Daphne, thinking hard of something really mad to say.

'Is your mother at home?'

'Mother approaches. Hark!' said Daphne,

30

putting one delicate little hand to her ear. She had just heard the heavy approaching tread of Lady Godolphin. Mrs Armitage was still prostrate abovestairs. The fact that she, Daphne, obviously did not know her own mother would surely confuse Mr Garfield and then convince him that she was truly mad.

Lady Godolphin came waddling in. She stopped short at the sight of Mr Garfield, her bulging eyes fastening almost greedily on his legs.

'I'm glad to see you're recovered,' she said. 'It is you, isn't it?'

'If you mean, am I the gentleman who was so very nearly killed by Mr Armitage's carelessness, then I am that gentleman.'

'You've cleaned up a treat,' said Lady Godolphin. 'Don't you think so, Daphne?'

'Who is a treat?' asked Daphne vaguely. Then she began to hum to herself, rocking backwards and forwards slightly on her chair.

'Mrs Armitage . . .' began Mr Garfield sternly.

'Don't Mrs Armitage me,' said Lady Godolphin. 'When I think of the sheer folly. Purging herself. Trying to clean her bowls with an excess of rhubarb pills. Follicles! She won't say so but she's trying to get thinner. Thin isn't fashionable, and so I told her. I've always been a good armful.' A wistful look crossed Lady Godolphin's face. 'My Arthur, that's Colonel Arthur Brian with whom I had an understanding but he ran off and left me for some Cit, well, he used to say it was as comforting as holding a feather pillow on a winter's night. He was always a bit of a poet, Arthur was.'

'Madame,' said Mr Garfield, putting up his glass. 'Am I to understand you are *not* Mrs Armitage?'

'Her name is Lady Godolphin,' said Daphne in a thin, high voice. She then looked sideways at Mr Garfield and rolled her eyes insanely, stuck her fingers in the corners of her mouth and pulled a horrible grimace.

Mr Garfield hurriedly averted his eyes. Godolphin, he thought. Of course! And Armitage. Now he remembered. This was the famous vicar who had successfully married off three beautiful daughters.

He felt suddenly dizzy and with a murmur of apology he sat down.

The physician had strongly advised him to rest in bed for three more days in order to recover fully from his concussion. But Mr Garfield had been so enraged at his treatment at the hands of the vicar, who he had damned as a cunning yokel, that he had been determined to leave. His head began to clear and he admitted ruefully to himself that part of his rage had been caused by loss of dignity.

Although he did not venture out much in society, Mr Garfield had already seen the three married Armitage sisters since they were invited everywhere.

While he recovered, Lady Godolphin studied him with interest. She had seen him before, of that she was sure.

'You have not introduced yourself, young man,' she said at last. 'But I am sure we have already met.'

'We did meet some time ago,' said Mr Garfield, searching his memory. Lady Godolphin. At last he remembered. She was much more subdued than the last time he had seen her when she had been wearing so much paint she had looked like

32

a particularly noisy sunset. She was accounted something of an eccentric, but definitely not insane. 'It was at the Courtlands', eight years ago,' he said. 'I came with Tommy Mercer. My name is Simon Garfield.'

How delighted Charles will be, thought Lady Godolphin cynically. That man does have the luck of the devil.

Probably singled him out for Daphne already. Garfield is as rich as Golden Ball. Richer! And a fine old family. One of those old families too grand to even bother to stoop to curry favour with royalty in order to get a title. But what on earth had come over Daphne? She looked half-witted.

Daphne had extracted some silks from her workbasket and was busily weaving the threads in her hair.

'Don't do that, Daphne,' said Lady Godolphin sharply. 'Anyone would think you was crazy.'

'Shall you be returning to town soon, my lady?' asked Mr Garfield, who thought Lady Godolphin a very cruel sort of person. There was no need to point out the girl was crazy when it was all too evident.

'I have only just arrived,' said Lady Godolphin. 'I'm rustyfacting.'

'Rusticating.'

'That's what I said.'

'Creditors?' suggested Mr Garfield tactfully.

'No, men.' Lady Godolphin sighed gustily. 'After me like wops round a honey pot. But I've given 'em up for Lent.'

'But Lent was some time ago.'

'Odso! But I am a very persistent person.'

Lady Godolphin sighed again and cast a roguish

look at Mr Garfield's legs.

'I have perhaps been too harsh on Mr Armitage,' said Mr Garfield. 'I threatened to take him to court for his carelessness but I have decided to forget the matter. It will, however, suit me very well if I never see him again.'

At that moment he looked across at Daphne and surprised a look of distinctly intelligent relief on that young lady's face.

Becoming aware of his gaze, Daphne immediately assumed an imbecilic look and started to weave the threads in her hair again. Lady Godolphin began to gossip about the thinness of company in London out of Season and the appalling condition of the drains. Mr Garfield listened and nodded while all the time his mind was busy. He had a feeling Daphne was acting. If so, why? But she had seemed so crazed, taking him for the bishop and asking for his blessing.

'Bishop,' he said suddenly. 'Miss Armitage mentioned a bishop. What bishop?'

Daphne began to sing very loudly indeed. 'Stop that row,' said Lady Godolphin, turning red. 'I'm surprised Charles told you, Mr Garfield, for he made us all swear to tell you you had imagined the whole thing.'

'What bishop?' repeated Mr Garfield.

'Why, the Bishop of Berham to be sure,' exclaimed Lady Godolphin. 'Stop winking like that, Daphne. Charles was told the bishop was calling to tell him to give up his pack, it not being a spiritual sport, so, as Charles told you, he went out and dug that pit in the road.'

Mr Garfield felt himself becoming very angry again. 'Do you mean to say that irresponsible vicar

34

dug a pit to stop his bishop's visit?'

'Oh, you *didn't* know,' said Lady Godolphin sadly, 'And now I've let the pig out of the poke. Charles *will* be mad.'

'I think you are *all* mad. Where is the vicar?'

'Gone to call on Squire Radford.'

Mr Garfield turned his yellow gaze on Daphne. 'I think I will wait until he gets back,' he said evenly.

A flicker of panic darted through Daphne's wide eyes, and then it was gone. She decided to escape and rose to her feet.

'Please tell Miss Armitage I would be delighted to enjoy the pleasure of her company until her father returns,' said Mr Garfield.

A predatory gleam appeared in Lady Godolphin's eyes. That Cyril Archer Daphne wished to wed was nothing more than a man-milliner. But this Mr Garfield, this *rich* Mr Garfield, had legs on him like an Adonis.

Lady Godolphin nodded. 'Sit down, Daphne,' she ordered, and Daphne, hearing the note of steel in her voice, miserably sat down.

*   *   *

'To say I am surprised and shocked would be to understate the matter,' said Squire Radford.

The Reverend Charles Armitage burrowed deeper into the depths of the comfortable armchair on one side of the squire's library fireplace, and mumbled, 'I'm leaving if you're going to jaw on and on.' It had been a relief to unburden himself to his old friend and he did not want to have to endure the subsequent lecture.

'Well, I've told you it all,' went on the vicar,

35

reaching out an arm and helping himself to another glass of port from the decanter on the table at his elbow. 'What stabs me is that this great pile o' moneybags is sittin' in my house. As sweet a windfall from the Marriage Mart as ever I did see. And there's my Daphne, the most beautiful girl in England. And this Garfield starts jawin' and sayin' he'll take me to court and instead of getting Daphne to soothe him down I called him a coxcomb. He probably didn't mean he would take me to court. Probably got a nasty knock on his cockloft that addled his wits.'

Squire Radford sighed. 'Charles,' he said in his high precise voice, 'you will need to face facts and the facts are as follows. Firstly, you cannot stop the bishop from visiting you by trying to murder him. Secondly, this Garfield is at outs with you. You must apologize most sincerely to him and tell him the *truth*. If you put your mind above mercenary motives, Charles, then things will come about.'

The vicar eyed his friend somewhat sourly. The squire was sitting in a high-backed chair facing him. He was a slight, elderly man, so small in stature that his old-fashioned buckled shoes barely touched the floor. He wore a bag wig, a black coat and black knee breeches. The vicar was very fond of Squire Jimmy Radford but at times found him too unworldly.

'You're right,' said the vicar at last. 'Tell you what . . we'll *both* go back and apologize to him.'

'But, my very dear Charles, *I* have nothing for which to apologize.'

'Just to help me, I meant. Sort of stand there *with* me while I say I'm sorry.'

The squire reluctantly agreed.

36

'That's noble of you, Jimmy,' said the vicar struggling out of the armchair. 'If we look penitent enough, mayhap he might decide to stay on and then he can marry Daphne.'

'Oh, Charles, you must make your apology sincere.'

'I will,' said the vicar. 'I sincerely want the Garfield money in the family so my 'pology will be the sincerest you've ever heard.'

The two friends decided to walk. The squire's pretty thatched cottage *ornée* stood on the far side of the village pond.

'Perhaps he will have left,' suggested the squire gently. 'I do not wish to admonish you, Charles, but . . .'

'Then don't,' said the vicar rudely.

The squire glanced at him sideways. The vicar's face was crumpled up in deep thought. Unlike Charles to be so mercenary when he was in funds, thought the squire. But the by-now famous marriages of his three eldest daughters had turned his head and he obviously thirsted to add another prize to that illustrious list he kept in the front of the family Bible.

Yellowhammers were calling from the hedgerows, 'A-little-bit-of-bread-and-*no*-cheese.' Starlings sent down their mocking, piping calls, and up on a chimney pot on the roof of The Six Jolly Beggarmen a blackbird launched into a rich melody. A slight breeze ruffled the water of the pond and farm labourers were beginning to come home from the fields.

The little squire felt uneasily that he should not have said he would accompany his friend. There was something so beautiful and tranquil and

37

spiritual about the peace of the evening, it seemed a pity to spoil it by becoming embroiled in the machinations of the earthy vicar.

The churchyard cross stood sharply up against the pale sky, a reminder of the good old days before gravestones when one memorial covered all the dead and a belief in eternal life with God was rather more important than the desire to be remembered in the sight of men.

The squire shivered. Sometimes death felt very close. He would like his name writ large on his tombstone. It was only human to dread disappearing from the world without having left even one little mark on it. Perhaps, mused the squire, the attraction that Charles Armitage held for him was because the vicar was so ebullient, so attached to the earth and fields, so very much part of the living.

But unknown to the squire, the peace of the evening had touched the vicar. He, Charles Armitage, was about to do a very noble thing. All at once he decided he did not care one way or the other for the rich Mr Garfield. As they turned into the lane leading to the vicarage, Mr Armitage promised his God that he would no longer think of money where his daughters were concerned. If this Cyril Archer were at all possible as a husband then Daphne could have him.

The vicar turned his calm face up to the sky and for him the angels sang.

Then he lowered his eyes and saw a strange carriage standing outside the vicarage and he knew in his bones that while he had been talking to Jimmy Radford, the bishop had arrived. The bishop had tricked him with tales of gout and was now waiting to demand that the vicar's hunting days be over.

'Rot him!' said the vicar passionately.

'Who!' exclaimed the squire.

'Dr Philpotts, that's who. Can't be anyone else.'

'Perhaps not,' said the squire soothingly. 'Perhaps one of your daughters has travelled to . . .'

'Not in any antiquated old carriage like that,' grumbled the vicar. 'Only a cheese-paring, clutch-fisted, port-hoarding curmudgeon like Philpotts would own a carriage like that.'

With a groan, the vicar led the way into the vicarage. It was as he feared.

Dr Philpotts was sitting in the parlour, sipping wine and eating biscuits. Mrs Armitage had recovered from her latest Spasm and looked well on the way to having another. She was drooping on the sofa with a vinaigrette in one hand and a handkerchief in the other. Lady Godolphin was rolling her eyes up to the ceiling. Daphne was bent over her sewing, and Mr Garfield was leaning back in his chair, his hands thrust in his breeches pockets, and looking thoughtfully at Daphne's bent head.

In all his worry, the vicar found time to wonder why the usually impeccable Daphne had silk threads twisted through her hair.

'Ah, Armitage,' said Dr Philpotts in a pompous fussy manner. 'I am persuaded I have caught you out. I deliberately threw you off your guard by sending word that I was not coming.'

The vicar looked at him with dislike. Dr Philpotts was a small round man with a fat white face, large pale grey eyes and a large red mouth.

'But now I am here and you are here,' went on

Dr Philpotts, 'I will come to the point of my visit.'

'Then perhaps we may all be excused,' said Mr Garfield. 'You will wish to be private with Mr Armitage.'

'Not at all. Not at all,' beamed Dr Philpotts. 'Mr Armitage must be chastised, must be made to understand the meaning of true humility. When I beat my children, I always call in the servants to be witness to their humiliation. Painful but salutary.'

'Disgusting, I call it,' said Lady Godolphin.

'Exactly,' beamed Dr Philpotts, 'although I am persuaded you are too hard on Mr Armitage.'

'Weren't talking about him,' sniffed Lady Godolphin. 'You. Hippochrist!'

The bishop flinched nervously under Lady Godolphin's baleful stare. 'Ha, ha, my lady, we will have our little joke.'

'I ain't joking,' said Lady Godolphin. 'I wish you had broke your neck.'

The bishop decided to ignore her. 'Mr Armitage,' he said sternly. 'I have written to you asking you, nay *demanding* that you cease hunting, that you give up your pack of hounds.'

'Steady, Charles,' murmured the squire, for veins were beginning to swell on the vicar's forehead and he had turned an alarming colour.

There was something in the vicar's appearance that roused Daphne's maternal instincts. She was heart-sorry for her father. She thought he looked like a large sulky baby about to hold its breath and turn blue with rage.

Without knowing why she did it, she turned her eyes to Mr Simon Garfield for help.

Those strange, hooded, yellowish eyes met and held her own trapped. They studied intently the appeal in her own—and the intelligence.

The vicar opened his mouth to begin but Mr Garfield forestalled him.

'What a very great pity, my lord bishop,' he said languidly. 'I had no idea Mr Armitage was being forced to surrender his truly national reputation as a fine huntsman. But I fear if that is the case I can no longer bring myself to donate the thousand guineas to the church that I brought with me for the purpose.'

'A thousand guineas!' The bishop goggled at Mr Garfield.

Mr Garfield raised his quizzing glass and slowly studied the bishop from gaiters to sparse grey hair. 'Unfortunately, I now fear I must keep my money,' he drawled.

'But *why?*' asked the bishop.

'Because, my dear man, Mr Armitage has inspired many Corinthians like myself with the divine spark. He has led us to glory over the . . . er . . . hunting grounds of the soul. We are simple men who must have our religion brought to us in simple ways.'

'Nicely put,' approved the squire. 'Quite my own sentiments.'

'Oh, but I had no idea,' exclaimed the bishop with a deprecating wave of his plump, white hands. 'If Mr Armitage can bring such ri— I mean such notable members of the *ton* as yourself, Mr Garfield, to an appreciation of the finer shades of the spirit then I most certainly must withdraw my demand.'

The vicar's face had gone from rage to disbelief to outright joy.

Mrs Armitage, who had been paying absolutely

no attention to the conversation, languidly roused herself to summon the maid with the tea tray.

Daphne wondered hysterically whether her mother was ever alive to any situation.

'That is most generous and most magnanimous of you,' said the vicar, trying to seize Mr Garfield's hand. But Mr Garfield appeared not to see the vicar's hand.

Mrs Armitage retained some remnants of correct social behaviour and so she roused herself to talk at length to the bishop about the business of the parish. Mrs Armitage never knew very much about what was going on in the village, but what she did not know, she made up. The bishop was obviously disappointed that he was not going to be allowed to make the Reverend Armitage's life a misery, but warring with that was the joy of bearing off with him one thousand guineas.

The light was failing rapidly and although there was to be a full moon, the bishop at last announced his intention of taking his leave. Mr Garfield, also, said he must be leaving as he meant to return to his friends at Hopeminster. Relief lightened the spirits of the party. Lady Godolphin was delighted because she had taken the bishop in dislike, the vicar because he was to keep his pack, and Daphne, because she found Mr Garfield's presence disturbing and threatening.

'Well,' said Dr Philpotts, getting to his feet, 'I will be most grateful to take that sum of money you promised, Mr Garfield. It will be most welcome and . . .'

'I'm not giving it to *you*,' said Mr Garfield; raising one thin eyebrow. 'I thought I had made myself plain. The money is to go to Mr Armitage

42

for repairs to his church.'

For one brief moment a most unchristian look flitted across the fat, white features of the bishop, and then he forced his large red mouth into a smile, and only Daphne heard him mutter something about the wicked flourishing as the green bay tree.

'A word with you in private,' said Mr Garfield when the bishop had taken his leave.

The vicar felt uncomfortable. He had a feeling that Mr Garfield in private was not going to be so pleasant as Mr Garfield in public.

'Mr Radford will join us,' he said hurriedly. 'He knows all my business.'

'Alone, if you please,' said Mr Garfield gently.

I never could abide men with red hair, thought the vicar sulkily, although Mr Garfield's hair was brown with copper lights.

He gloomily led the way into his study and thrust aside the clutter of objects on his desk, and looked up somewhat mutinously at the tall figure of his guest whose broad shoulders seemed to fill the small room.

The vicar remembered his apology and straightened his fat back.

'Sit down, sit 'ee down,' he said, waving a chubby hand towards a chair. 'The fact is, I owe you a heartfelt apology and if you still want to take me to court over the matter, then I'll need to face that when it comes. I heard old Philpotts was coming for to tell me to get rid of my pack. Me! There ain't a pack in England to match mine outside the Quorn. It was a mortal hard blow to take and so I had that there pit dug in the road. Not to harm the old man in any way but just to give him a jolt. It was a stupid thing to do. I ask your forgiveness.'

'Very well. You have it,' said Mr Garfield. The vicar mopped his brow with a large belcher handkerchief and felt a spiritual glow of righteousness spreading through his body. Squire Radford's advice had been correct.

He had told the truth. He was not to be punished; in fact he was to be rewarded, since Mr Garfield meant to give him a thousand guineas. The vicar's small eyes filled with tears of gratitude.

'What brought you to Hopeworth?' asked the vicar.

'I was sent by a friend to purchase a couple hounds.'

'You shall have them,' said the vicar emotionally, 'and not one penny payment shall I accept.'

'If they were for me,' pointed out Mr Garfield, 'then I should certainly accept your kind offer. But since they are not, I insist on paying a fair price for them.'

'There must be some other way I can repay you,' said the vicar anxiously.

'Oh, there is,' replied Mr Garfield equably. 'Shall we visit the kennels first?'

Overjoyed that the day had turned out so well, the vicar lit a lantern and led the way around the house to the kennels.

'Your daughter, Daphne,' said Mr Garfield abruptly as he cast an eye over the sleepy hounds who had just had their evening meal. 'She is not lacking in intelligence, I trust?'

'No,' said the startled vicar. 'She ain't a bluestocking, thanks be to God.'

'But not lacking any of her mental faculties?'

'See here,' said the vicar acidly. 'It's the points o' the hounds you're supposed to be going over.'

44

'Yes. But I will return to the matter of your daughter in a little while.'

The vicar looked up at him nervously. This Garfield couldn't be interested in Daphne? Not after that prayer that he, the Reverend Armitage, had sent up to the heavens.

It almost seemed like a bad omen when Mr Garfield at last selected Bellsire and Thunderer.

For unlike Diana and Frederica, the soft-hearted Daphne was apt to make a pet of the dogs. Not that she ever allowed them to spread hairs on her gown, but sometimes she would stroke them after feeding time and talk nonsense to them when she thought no one was around.

The vicar had been rather touched by the pretty sight one evening when he had found his impeccable daughter murmuring softly to the noisy dogs.

Bellsire and Thunderer were Daphne's favourites.

Biting his lip, the vicar called for John Summer and told him to put the hounds in Mr Garfield's carriage.

It was unfortunate that Daphne should emerge from the house just at that moment.

'You are not sending Bellsire and Thunderer away, Papa!' she cried. 'They are little more than puppies.'

The two foxhounds cavorted about her. Their ears had not yet been rounded and their white and tan coats gleamed with health.

Mr Garfield noticed with amusement that the beautiful Miss Daphne now had all her wits about her and was not even attempting to hide the fact.

'Mr Garfield has chosen them, Daphne,' said the

45

vicar, 'and it is the least we can do for him after his generosity.'

'They are not for me,' said Mr Garfield. 'They are for a friend of mine, a Mr Edwin Apsley.'

'And is Mr Apsley *kind* to animals?'

'Miss Daphne, he wishes a couple of hounds for his pack, not for the drawing room.'

Daphne's long preserved calm finally broke. 'I am persuaded he will ill-treat them if he is a Corinthian like yourself. He will *whip* them!'

'Daphne!' howled the vicar. 'Go to your room!'

Daphne, for once unmindful of her dress, was kneeling in the gravel, hugging both dogs who were licking her face.

At her father's words, tears started to her eyes, and she gave a gulping sob, got to her feet and ran into the house.

'Come into the study, Mr Garfield,' said the vicar gruffly. 'Was ever a man so plagued? You wouldn't get my other girls sentimentalizing over a pair o' animals. I'm amazed at Daphne. I've never seen her this put about before. Always the quietest and most biddable of girls.'

A price was agreed on and Mr Garfield rose to take his leave.

Reluctantly the vicar reminded Mr Garfield that he had said there was some way in which he might be repaid for all his kindness.

'Do you bring your daughter to London?' asked Mr Garfield abruptly.

'Daphne? She's just returned. Was staying with Lady Brabington, Annabelle, her sister,' said the vicar, walking to the window and peering out at the purple night pricked by the first twinkling stars.

The vicar remembered his prayer. 'Fact is,' he

46

said cautiously, 'Daphne met some fellow when she was last up and talked about an engagement . . . to a Mr Archer.'

'Cyril Archer?'

'The same.'

Mr Garfield swung around. 'I am persuaded they would not suit. I know this Mr Archer.'

'But my dear sir . . .'

'I did not ask you for your daughter's hand in marriage,' said Mr Garfield evenly, 'I only asked you for your help in furthering my acquaintance with her.'

'So you did,' said the vicar, brightening visibly. He looked up fondly at the tall figure of Mr Garfield, seeing in his place sacks and sacks of guineas. 'I'll do my best.'

'Thank you. I will now take my leave of yourself and Mrs Armitage.'

Mr Garfield had the opportunity of meeting the vicar's two youngest daughters. Diana he considered unfortunately mannish, and little Frederica was a plain, wispy thing. There was no sign of the glorious Daphne. Mrs Armitage extended her hand in a swan-like way and murmured apologies for the lack of hospitality 'for we are at such sixes and sevens. I declare servants get more difficult to manage each year.'

Behind her, the maid, Betty, scowled darkly. Lady Godolphin extended an invitation to one of her salons and cast a last loving look at his legs. And then he was gone.

'Drat!' exclaimed the vicar. 'I never got that thousand guineas.'

'I think he only said it to help you escape the bishop,' pointed out Lady Godolphin.

'I don't know what came over Daphne,' went on the vicar. 'Thank goodness you're sensible when it comes to animals, Diana.'

'I wouldn't dream of making such a missish scene,' said Diana proudly, but inside she felt an ache at her heart. Bellsire and Thunderer had been the clowns of the pack, funny and noisy and always up to mischief. She thought of them under the lash of a strange master and felt her eyes fill with tears.

'Mr Radford has departed,' said Mrs Armitage. 'What an exhausting day. Betty, make me a tisane. I must lie down.'

The vicar was glad Squire Radford had gone home, otherwise he might have been tempted to blurt out Mr Garfield's interest in Daphne, and Jimmy Radford would look at him severely and accuse him of being mercenary.

Rubbing his hands, the vicar went into the house. He would write to Mr Garfield as soon as that gentleman's carriage which had been damaged in the bishop-trap was repaired and perhaps delicately remind him of the money he had promised to give the church.

Best handle Daphne carefully. Best get her to London soon. Perhaps he might go himself, thought the vicar, and have a word in the ear of this pesky Mr Archer.

While Daphne cried herself to sleep upstairs, the vicar sat downstairs and planned her wedding to Simon Garfield.

CHAPTER THREE

Mr Garfield was glad to return to the well-ordered sanity of his friend's mansion. He had the dogs sent ahead to London where no doubt Mr Apsley, if he could wrench himself away from his latest inamorata, would transfer them to his own kennels in the country.

He stayed on for two weeks at Hopeminster because he was suffering from headaches and not yet fully recovered from his accident.

It was the end of August when he at last made his way back to his town house in Albemarle Street. For the first time since his visit to Hopeworth, he remembered he had not honoured his promise of the gift of one thousand guineas to the village church. He sent for his secretary, Harold Evans, and gave him instructions to find some individual capable of organizing the restoration of a church. Mr Garfield wanted to make sure his money went on the purpose for which it was meant and not straight into the reverend's pocket.

There were many invitations waiting for him although the Little Season was not yet begun. He was about to tell his secretary to refuse them all, when he decided to examine them instead. As he expected, there was one from Lady Godolphin inviting him to a dinner. The dinner was to be held that very evening. Probably her ladyship would not expect him to turn up. And yet . . .

'Send a footman round to Lady Godolphin's,' he told Mr Evans, 'and say I shall be delighted to attend this evening unless she has already found a substitute for me.'

He carefully went through his correspondence, dealing with business matters, personal letters, and several hundred requests for money.

Then he ordered all his tradesmen's bills to be paid promptly—a most ungentlemanly procedure—after which he decided to go out and call on his friend Mr Apsley.

At the back of his mind, Mr Garfield had some idea he might find Daphne Armitage at Lady Godolphin's dinner, and, therefore, it would only be polite to assure that young lady of the hounds' welfare.

He was, of course, quite sure he did not have serious intentions as far as Daphne Armitage was concerned. For the moment, the idea of her amused him, and Mr Garfield was very rarely amused.

At times he envied his friends who seemed capable of being quite happy with the daily fashionable round. Edwin Apsley, for example, followed the pattern of Rowlandson's *Man of Fashion*.

'Queer dreams, owing to Sir Richard's claret, always drink too much of it—rose at one—dressed by half-past three—took an hour's ride—a good horse, my last purchase, remember to sell him again—nothing like variety—dined at six with Sir Richard—said several good things—forgot 'em all—in high spirits—quizzed a parson—drank three bottles, and lounged to the theatre—not quite clear about the play—comedy or tragedy—forget which—saw the last act—Kemble toll loll—not quite certain whether it was Kemble or not—Mrs Siddons monstrous fine—got into a hack—set

50

down in St James's Street—dipp'd a little with the boys at hazards—confounded bad luck—lost all my money.'

The hour being two in the afternoon, Mr Garfield was confident of finding his friend still at breakfast and so he made his way in the direction of Mr Apsley's lodgings.

Because Mr Apsley was perpetually out of pocket he lived off the Tottenham Court Road, claiming that since he invariably ate his dinner at other people's houses and never entertained, he might as well save his blunt by paying for modest lodgings. Money was needed for more important things like hazard or horses.

The day was uncomfortably warm and a small sun glared down through the haze of smoke from a brassy sky. The streets were alive with the sounds of the street vendors. Baking apples sold by old women and cooked on a charcoal stove at the street corner lent a welcome hot spice to the foul air. A man with a donkey was selling brick dust for cleaning knives, his voice high and strident. Strapping Welsh women still went on their milk rounds, their heavy pails slung on a wooden yoke across the shoulders.

Lavender, grown near London at Mitcham, was being sold in fragrant bunches. Every housewife had some for the linen press since the washing soap stank so abominably.

'Bellows to mend,' yelled a wrinkled gnome who seemed to have materialized at Mr Garfield's elbow. His head began to ache again and he wished heartily he had not decided to walk.

At the corner of the Tottenham Court Road, he had to step around a vociferous orange seller

51

who was offering a 'Bill of the play' with every six oranges bought. Awful things those playbills were, made from long flimsy strips of tissue paper, wet from the printers, smearing the hands with black ink which never seemed to have time to dry since there was a fresh play every evening.

Mr Garfield picked his way through the jostling crowd, past McQueen's Buildings, past the Leopard Coffee House, past the Dunbar iron foundry and on to the corner of Francis Street.

Mr Apsley lived in a top floor flat in number thirty-two. The stairway was dusty and smelled of dry rot and drains, but it was a haven of quiet after the clamour outside.

Mr Garfield mounted. the steps two at a time, feeling the nagging, throbbing pain in his head increasing. All at once he wondered if the blow to his head had damaged his brains. Here he was, out on a hot and dusty day to check on the welfare of two foxhounds, all to please a young lady who liked him so little she had pretended to be mad, and furthermore was the daughter of an eccentric vicar whose plot against his bishop was the sole reason that he, Simon Garfield, was suffering from a confounded headache.

He rapped on Mr Apsley's door with unnecessary vigour and was rewarded with a volley of barking and the scrabble of paws against the door on the other side.

The door swung open. Bellsire and Thunderer threw themselves against Mr Garfield, whimpering and slavering, and behind them, cutting at their stems with a whip, was an enraged Mr Apsley.

'I'll kill those curst hell hounds,' he roared. 'Look what they've done, dammit.'

He reached behind him and held up a mangled and chewed hessian boot.

Mr Garfield leaned wearily against the door jamb.

'Can't you take these animals inside, Edwin?' he said. 'My head aches like the very deuce. What on earth are you doing with these animals in London? They should be in the country.'

'I'll kill the pair o' them,' roared Mr Apsley, taking another cut at Thunderer's rear. Thunderer showed the whites of his eyes and forced his way between Mr Garfield's legs, seeking refuge.

Mr Garfield twitched the whip from his friend's grasp and threw it down the stairwell.

'*Now* will you pay attention, Edwin? Am I to stand here all day while you shout and cavort? Leave the whoresons of hounds alone and let me inside so that I may sit down and drink a glass of wine.'

'Been drinking deep,' said Mr Apsley sympathetically. 'Got just the thing for it.'

He led the way into a cluttered living room. Mr Apsley was wearing a morning cap and a banyan, that comfortable cotton house-gown so beloved by members of the *ton*. A stocky, cheerful young man, he made up for what he lacked in intellect by being almost generally good-natured. He had dusty fair hair and a snub nose in a round face which was his private despair. No amount of pinching or pulling seemed able to bring it up to Mr Garfield's aristocratic prominence.

Simon Garfield sank gratefully into a chair. Both hounds crept under it. 'What's this?' he asked as Mr Apsley handed him a mud-coloured drink.

'No heel taps,' grinned Mr Apsley. 'Tell you

after.'

Mr Garfield took a large gulp and then placed his glass carefully on the table. 'What is this filth?' he enquired pleasantly.

'Brandy and buttermilk. Nothing like it.'

Mr Garfield sighed. 'You are quite right. There isn't. Pour me a glass of hock and seltzer, there's a good fellow, and tell me why you are lashing these poor animals. You are not normally so bad-tempered. Has your fair lady left you?'

'That seems to be it in a nutshell,' agreed Mr Apsley gloomily. 'Greedy little charmer, she was. But such shoulders! Got to send these hounds off.'

'They are perfectly good foxhounds,' said Mr Garfield. 'They were in prime condition when I gave them to you. Now I remark that they are frightened, their coats are dull, they lack exercise, and they do not look as if they have been fed.'

'They'll be right as rain when I get them down to the country,' said Mr Apsley.

'No, I do not think so,' said Mr Garfield quietly. He took a sip of the glass of hock and seltzer his friend had just given him and half-closed his eyes.

Mr Apsley glanced at the clock and gave a start. 'Ods Niggins! I've got to be in Cavendish Square in half an hour and my man is out on an errand. Well, I'll need to dress myself. Ah, the trials of fashion. You do seem worried about those wretched animals.'

'I would not treat a horse the way you treat those animals,' said Mr Garfield severely. 'You must not take out your unrequited love on dumb foxhounds.'

'Look, you *are* upset,' called Mr Apsley from the bedroom. 'I'll feed 'em and pet 'em and send 'em off tonight.'

54

Bellsire crept out from under the chair and put a large paw on Mr Garfield's knee.

'Down,' he commanded sternly. 'No, my dear Edwin,' he said raising his voice, 'I must inform you I am buying these hounds back. In fact, since you have not yet given me the money for them, I regard them as my own.'

'Then *have* 'em,' came Mr Apsley's cheerful voice. 'Can't stand the beasts.'

Strange, mused Mr Garfield, absently stroking Thunderer's ears as the dog poked his head out and rested it on Mr Garfield's boot, that one really does not know one's friends. I never would have thought old Edwin a vicious sort of fellow, and yet his treatment of two fine foxhounds is callous in the extreme, not to say downright silly, since they are valuable dogs.

He blinked slightly as Mr Apsley finally emerged in all the glory of the costume of the Four in Hand Club. He was wearing a blue single-breasted coat with a long waist, ornamented with brass buttons engraved with the words 'Four in Hand Club'. Under it, he sported a waistcoat of kerseymere ornamented with alternate stripes of blue and yellow. His small clothes were of white corduroy, made moderately high, and very long over the knee, buttoning in front over the shin bone.

His boots were very short with long tops, only one outside strap to each, and one to the back; the latter were employed to keep the breeches in their proper longitudinal shape. His hat had a conical crown and an Allen brim. Over it all, he wore a box coat of white drab cloth with fifteen capes, two tiers of pockets, and an inside one for a Belcher handkerchief. His cravat was of white muslin spotted with black. As a finishing touch, he thrust a bouquet of pink geraniums in his buttonhole.

'You will die of the heat,' pointed out Mr Garfield, 'and I thought those buttons were out of fashion. Queen Anne shillings are the thing, dear boy.'

'I'm bringing 'em in again,' said Mr Apsley triumphantly. 'I won't feel the heat once I set my team in motion.'

Mr Garfield picked up two dog leashes from the table and snapped his fingers. Thunderer and Bellsire crept out. He fastened the leashes to the dogs' collars and rose to find Mr Apsley surveying him with awkward embarrassment.

'I say, Simon,' ventured Mr Apsley. 'You ain't thinking of promenading through the streets of London with two foxhounds?'

'No,' said Mr Garfield equably. 'You will be driving us.'

'Won't do. What if my Kitty should see us? No, no, Simon. If you want to make a cake of yourself, do it without my presence. I would never live it down. Why, I wouldn't be invited anywhere! Now you, you don't go anywhere so it's not the same.'

'You amaze me, Edwin. Not only are you cruel to animals, you are extremely egotistical, and have the manners of a Cit.'

'Oh, I say, you ain't *serious*?'

'Probably not,' sighed Mr Garfield. 'My head aches and I am so very hot. Here comes your man. Do not trouble to show me out. I shall precede you with my obnoxious hounds. Belsire, Thunderer. Come!'

The dogs meekly followed him from the apartment and quietly negotiated the long flight of

56

stairs. Once out in the street, they showed alarming signs of being about to leap about the whole of the Tottenham Court Road with sheer joy at their deliverance.

'Dog's meat!' shouted a man cheerfully. 'Prime dog's meat, guv. Horse flesh, bullock's livers, tripe cuttings.'

Mr Garfield gathered the leashes in one hand and raised a scented handkerchief to his nose with the other.

'Two pounds of whatever you please,' he said faintly. He paid the required price of fivepence and went on his way with the dogs panting at his heels, leading the way through the network of streets which approached Piccadilly.

Along Piccadilly strolled the impeccable Mr Garfield, oblivious to the raised quizzing glasses and startled stares of the *ton*.

He made his way into the Green Park where he spread the package of dog's meat out on the grass. 'I should have it cooked,' he said, 'but you are probably hungry enough to eat it raw.'

The dogs fell on the meat while Mr Garfield settled himself on an iron park bench and fished his cheroot box out of his pocket. The two dogs finished their meal in record time and then lay panting in the sun, their tongues lolling out.

Mr Garfield sat and smoked and wondered whether he should risk enduring an evening at Lady Godolphin's. There was no real reason to believe that Daphne Armitage would be in town. But he had expressed an interest in furthering his acquaintance with her and that should be enough to spur on any parent, particularly one as avaricious as he had sensed the vicar to be. Mr Garfield had been hunted down by ambitious parents from the day he had come into his inheritance. He had summed up the reverend as being an extremely mercenary man. Poor Daphne was probably hustled off to London the day after his departure.

Daphne, who would by now have been made aware of his power and fortune, would no longer fascinate him by pretending to be mad but would simper and giggle and flirt like all the other girls who had bored him so much in the past.

Everything in London seemed to be exhausted by the long drought of summer. He could not even remember when it had last rained. The grass was parched and dusty and the leaves of the trees rustled metallically in the dry breeze. There was to be a Grand Review of Volunteers in Hyde Park on the morrow. Perhaps he might invite Miss Armitage, if Miss Armitage did not prove as tedious as he was sure she would turn out to be.

At last he rose and collected his charges and made his leisurely way home with the happy dogs, full of food, stumbling at his heels.

He would have banished them to the kitchens but they looked so cowed and terrified that he impatiently ordered his servants to let them stay.

At last he stepped out into the hot, still evening, dressed in his best. He wore a severely cut black dress coat with silver buttons over a white piqué waistcoat. His pantaloons of fawn stockinette fitted his legs like a second skin.

His copper hair was cut *à la Titus* and he wore his cravat in the Osbaldiston. Although he was often pointed out as a notable Corinthian because of his expertise at all sorts of sport, Mr Garfield did not affect the Tom and Jerry fashions of the other

Corinthians who seemed determined to look as if they had just left the stables.

He stood calmly waiting for his carriage and trying to ignore the howls of canine anguish which were filling the house behind him.

He was not a hunting man and began to worry whether foxhounds were more sensitive than other breeds. He wondered insanely whether they might go into a decline.

What if Miss Armitage should prove that wonderful being for whom he had searched so long—a woman who would not bore him after ten minutes? And what if she asked after those wretched beasts and he had to confess they had died of broken hearts?

His carriage arrived and two of his footmen marched forwards to let down the steps and open the door.

'James,' said Mr Garfield, drawing on his gloves, 'pray go into the house and fetch the dogs. I am taking them with me.'

James cast an eloquent look at the carriage, which was an open barouche.

'Very good, sir,' he said woodenly.

Mr Garfield settled himself in the carriage and sighed.

The door of the house opened and Thunderer and Bellsire streaked out, tugging the helpless footman after them.

'Sit!' commanded Mr Garfield awfully. The dogs climbed up on the seat next to him and sat up very straight, looking around them eagerly, their pink tongues lolling out.

'I say,' said Lord Hazleton anxiously to his friend the Honourable John Jakes. 'Ain't that Garfield, and ain't he got two foxhounds?'

Mr Jakes tried not to stare. 'Pon rep,' he giggled. 'You are not up to the mark. Foxhounds is In. Everybody takes a couple around.'

Each man strolled on, privately wondering how soon they could find a couple to rival Mr Garfield.

*   *   *

The Reverend Charles Armitage was a most discontented man. He had brought Daphne to London shortly after Mr Garfield's visit with all the speed of a man long-accustomed to rushing his daughters up and down to town in pursuit of various marriageable beaux. He had been astounded by the fact that Mrs Armitage had briefly emerged into the real world to show some animation at the prospect of Daphne's alliance with Mr Garfield and had announced her intention of coming to London as well. Minerva was still in Brighton giving her two-year-old son, Julian, the benefit of the sea air, and so the Armitage family were making use of her husband Lord Sylvester Comfrey's town house.

Diana was sulking and pining and complaining that she did not like life in town and London smelled abominably.

Little Frederica seemed to have her nose in some book or other and could rarely be persuaded to step out of doors.

The vicar had strolled past Mr Garfield's house from time to time in the hope of seeing some sign that that gentleman had returned, but to date he seemed noticeably absent.

Annabelle showed little interest in the prospect of Daphne making a rich marriage. She played all day long with baby Charles and did not seem to pay much attention to her husband.

And then there was the beautiful Mr Archer. The vicar had dropped several very large hints in that exquisite young man's shell-like ear that he would not be a welcome addition to the Armitage family, but Mr Archer had just smiled sweetly at the vicar and had said something quite inane which showed he had not been paying the slightest attention whatsoever.

Then there was Daphne herself. Never had she looked more beautiful or had she appeared more lifeless. Which all went to show, thought the vicar savagely, that Cyril Archer was doing nothing to raise her spirits at all. She most certainly was not in love with the man.

In that, he was wrong. For Daphne had persuaded herself she was in love with Mr Archer; persuaded herself with such intensity that it was almost the same as the real thing. Once again, however, she carefully controlled her manner and expression. If she just went doggedly on with the goal of marriage to Mr Archer in mind, neither looking to the right nor the left, then things would work out. She and Mr Archer could set up house somewhere pretty and admire each other at length. Mr Archer did not expect her to think very deeply on any subject and would have been quite alarmed if Daphne had shown any signs of animation or intelligence. Deep down Daphne sensed this, and since she herself found Mr Archer's calm and beautiful stupidity an attraction, she was well able to appreciate the value of her own attraction for him and take pains not to do anything to mar it.

She was glad the irritating and upsetting Mr

61

Garfield had stayed away. From time to time she worried about Bellsire and Thunderer, imagining them being ill-treated, cursed and beaten. Sometimes she even fantasized finding out the direction of Mr Apsley's kennels and rescuing the hounds on a dark moonless night.

Mr Archer had called on her that very afternoon and had taken her for a drive in the park. Her father had been absent and Mrs Armitage could find nothing amiss in allowing the seemingly innocuous Mr Archer to squire her daughter. It had been a pleasant and undemanding outing and they had excited a great deal of admiration. Mr Archer was divinely fair with white gold curls falling over a broad marble brow. His eyes were of a deep and intense blue and his mouth was beautifully shaped and perpetually curled in one of those smiles you see on classical statues—which is really what it was in a way, Mr Archer having practised that smile before the looking glass until he had it quite perfect.

He had rather curved elongated lids as well which added to his classical appearance. His only fault was that he was rather hollow-chested but that had been rectified by buckram wadding, and, since Daphne had never seen him without his coat, she was unaware of this defect.

Lady Godolphin had been thrown into a flurry by the arrival of Mr Garfield's footman for she *had* found a substitute for him to make up her dinner table, that substitute being the fair Mr Archer. She knew Mr Armitage would be annoyed but she had always considered Mr Archer merely as a decoration and no threat at all.

In despair, Lady Godolphin had sent a note to

Mr Archer's lodgings, telling him that unfortunately his presence would mean she would be seating thirteen and she did so hope he would not consider it inconvenient to consider his invitation null and void.

Mr Archer had sent a note by return saying, yes, he did find it inconvenient and looked forward to her dinner party prodigiously, which made Lady Godolphin so incensed she damned him as having a hide as thick as a runningsoris.

But at least Lady Godolphin had the pleasure of letting Mr Armitage know that the prey in the form of Mr Garfield was shortly to enter the net.

The vicar's spirits soared again but caution prevented him from telling Daphne that Mr Garfield was to be one of the guests.

Daphne knew that Archer was to be at Lady Godolphin's and so Daphne would no doubt be looking her most beautiful.

Daphne did look exquisite as the Armitage party set out for Lady Godolphin's. Only Daphne, Mr and Mrs Armitage were to attend. Diana and Frederica, to their great relief, were to be left behind. Daphne was wearing a white muslin gown with a thin gold stripe, each stripe having been delicately embroidered onto the fine fabric. The dress had a very high waist and a very low bodice. The bodice was unlined and the thin material exposed more of Daphne's charms to the public gaze than the vicar thought seemly.

The trouble was he only noticed the scantiness of her gown when they arrived at Lady Godolphin's. He also noticed that the gown opened all the way down the back to reveal a pink scanty petticoat which managed to create the fleeting illusion that

63

Daphne was wearing nothing underneath.

The vicar's conscience told him he should ask Lady Godolphin to lend Daphne a shawl. But the other Mr Armitage fought stoutly with the niggling voice of conscience—and won. Girls were fit for nothing better in life than to get married and rear children, and if you were going to bait the man-trap, then it argued that the bait should be as attractive as possible.

Daphne had chosen the dress some time ago from a fashion plate in *La Belle Assemblée*. She was not in the slightest aware that it was daring; only that it felt cool and comfortable and that the gold and white nicely set off the blackness of her hair and the whiteness of her skin.

She was completely unaware of the sexual attractions of her body; she was only conscious of the beauty of her face.

In Mr Archer's inclusion in the dinner party, Daphne saw great hope. Her father's moods were as variable as the winds of Heaven, and given that the wind was blowing in the right direction at the right time, then it was quite possible that she would be able to marry Mr Archer and live placidly ever after.

It was not until the company was gathered in Lady Godolphin's Green Saloon that Mrs Armitage let the cat out of the bag. She tweaked Daphne's dress at the back to straighten the fall of the delicate muslin and murmured, 'I am glad you are in looks, my pet. Mr Garfield is a very great catch.'

'Oh, mama, Mr Garfield is not here,' pointed out Daphne, smiling in an unruffled way in the direction of Mr Archer.

'But he is expected!' said Mrs Armitage.

A tide of colour rushed into Daphne's face. She remembered Mr Garfield's hard mouth, hard body, and strange yellow eyes. All at once she felt her security threatened and instinctively moved to Mr Archer's side.

'Your dress is beautiful, Miss Daphne,' said that gentleman. 'I must copy that idea for a waistcoat—gold stripes on white muslin.'

'Do but listen!' hissed Daphne. 'Mr Simon Garfield is shortly to arrive and Papa wishes me to marry him.'

'But you cannot,' said Mr Archer simply, 'for *we* are to be married—to each other.'

Daphne felt let down. If this was a proposal of marriage, it was not the sort of proposal of which she had dreamt.

'*Are* we to be married?' she whispered, but Mr Archer had found a loose thread in the discreet length of striped stocking which was peeping below his left pantaloon leg and that seemed to be absorbing all his attention, as in fact it was. He was wondering whether to boldly demand a pair of scissors to snip off the offending thread, or whether to make an excuse and retire to his lodgings and do it there, or whether his nails were sharp enough to slice it off, or whether, if he tugged it, the whole stocking would bunch up into an unseemly knot.

There was no one of very great moment at the dinner party—for alas poor Brummell, fled to the Continent before his baying creditors—and London was thin of company. Mr Archer had now heard Mr Garfield was to be of the party but was not impressed. Any man who did not cultivate the good will of the *ton* was beyond his understanding and no one had ever seen Mr Garfield trying to impress anyone.

It showed Lady Godolphin's current lack of spirit in that the guests, other than the three Armitages, Mr Archer, and the still absent Mr Garfield, were all comparatively young, Lady Godolphin normally liking to surround herself with septuagenarians so that she might feel young herself. There were three married couples, Lord and Lady Brothers, the Honourable Peter and Mrs Nash, and Colonel and Mrs Cartwright, all of unimpeachable social standing, all thirtyish, and all infernally dull.

Conversation turned on the enormous size of the Prince Regent which had prompted a solemn article in *The Times* about how he contrived to mount a horse.

'An inclined plane,' that august newspaper had reported, 'was constructed, rising to the height of two feet and a half, at the upper end of which was a platform. His Royal Highness was placed on a chair on rollers, which was then raised by screws high enough to let the horse pass under; and finally, his Royal Highness was let gently down into the saddle. By these means the Regent was undoubtedly able to enjoy in some degree the benefit of air and exercise . . .'

But Lord Brothers shook his head and said that even that device had failed to tempt the Regent into the saddle of late since he had left off his stays and was become Falstaffian in bulk and language. 'He told me t'other day when I was at Brighton,' confided Lord Brothers, 'that even the fineness of weather does not tempt him abroad. His great size and weight make him nervous and he is afraid to ride. He says, "Why should I? I never had better spirits, appetite and health than when I stay within, and I am not so well when I go abroad."'

Mrs Nash, who was of a sour disposition, said that the Regent was entirely given over to pleasure and idleness and spent most of his days shut up with his tailors examining different patterns of uniforms.

Colonel Cartwright said acidly that the whole conversation smacked of sedition and for his part he had found the Regent to be very hard-working. Since he glared quite ferociously around the room as he said this, it had the effect of causing an awkward silence.

Then Lady Godolphin weighed in with, 'I *do* think His Highness's idea of throwing open *all* the prisons and asylums next Sunday is such a *good* and humane idea. Do you think it will work out?'

The shocked babble and exclamations that greeted this whopping lie had the desired effect of getting everyone to talk again.

And then, above the noise, the butler announced loudly and clearly, 'Mr Garfield.'

Daphne found her heart beginning to beat very hard and moved very close to Mr Archer. Her father glared at her furiously but she pretended not to notice.

Mr Archer began to murmur fretfully in Daphne's ear, 'I wonder where he got that waistcoat. White piqué! But don't you find it a trifle severe?'

Daphne did not appear to have heard him. She was watching Simon Garfield as he moved from group to group until at last he stood before her.

'Miss Daphne,' he murmured, 'how very beautiful you look. And with all your wits about you which most definitely adds to your charm.'

'Thank you, sir,' said Daphne calmly, not one

flicker of expression marring the smooth oval of her face.

Mr Garfield's gaze dropped for a second to her bosom and a strange yellow light turned his eyes to topaz. Then his eyes returned to Daphne's bland face and he gave a little sigh as if something had disappointed him.

The vicar was standing behind Mr Garfield, hopping from foot to foot in his impatience. He wanted Daphne to rouse herself and do something to attract Mr Garfield. He also wanted to remind Mr Garfield about his promise of one thousand guineas.

At last Mr Garfield turned around and surveyed the little vicar. 'I have asked my secretary to find an expert to restore your church, Mr Armitage,' he said.

'No need for that, don't you see,' pointed out the vicar eagerly. 'We have local craftsmen a-plenty.'

'No doubt,' said Mr Garfield. 'But they will need someone to direct them. You amaze me, reverend. I would have supposed you delighted not only to have the money but to have the organization of the matter taken out of your hands.'

'Oh, well,' muttered the vicar. 'Very kind of you, I'm sure.'

Mr Garfield bowed before his baffled look and made his way towards his hostess.

'Very pleased you could honour us,' said Lady Godolphin and then spoiled her courteous remark by adding sourly, 'It weren't for want o' trying. I sent card after card.'

'The honour is mine,' said Mr Garfield. 'I am amazed you went to so much trouble to ensure my presence.'

68

'Nagged into it, and that's a fact.'

'Indeed. By whom?'

'Oh, never mind,' said Lady Godolphin, cursing her own loose tongue. She rang the bell. What on earth had happened to dinner?

Her worry grew as her butler, Mice, failed to answer the summons. Footmen were circulating with glasses of wine, lemonade and ratafia. 'If this evening is successful,' thought Lady Godolphin, 'then I shall charge the lot to Charles.'

Mindful of her promise to help the Armitages, she turned back to Mr Garfield.

'Miss Daphne is in looks, would you say?' she asked.

'Very much so,' remarked Mr Garfield with pleasant indifference.

'Not gettin' married?' pursued Lady Godolphin.

'I am a happy bachelor, my lady, I have no ambitions in that direction. Have you?'

Lady Godolphin blinked, and then realised he had probably a right to be equally personal. 'No,' she sighed. 'I have decided to remain chased and unsulkied. Drat that man. Mice.'

'Some gentleman is responsible for a plague of mice?'

'No, no, my butler, Mice. What ails the man?'

Mr Garfield helped himself to another glass of madeira and watched with amusement as Lady Godolphin's angry eyes looked pointedly at his glass and then pointedly at the vicar as if hammering home how much it was all costing.

Mr Garfield glanced at Mr Archer and he wondered if Daphne knew what she was about in that direction. Did she think Mr Archer really the beautiful, rather effeminate man he seemed?

Probably she did. There had been a few unsavoury stories about him but they were not in general circulation.

Perhaps they deserved each other. It was a pity that such a beautiful girl should turn out to be so insipid. Mr Archer bent his head and said something. Daphne caught Mr Garfield's watching eye and, yes, she definitely simpered.

The double doors leading to the saloon opened and the butler appeared, hurriedly straightening his striped waist-coat.

'Dinner is served,' he said in a strangled falsetto. 'Been at the port again,' mumbled Lady Godolphin.

The party filed across the hall to the dining room in order of precedence.

Daphne had the honour of being seated next to Mr Garfield at dinner.

She had caught his fleeting look of disgust when she had quite deliberately simpered in that silly way and so decided to be as missish as possible.

The first course was green pea soup removed by a haunch of lamb, larded and glazed with cucumber sauce.

Lady Godolphin did not believe in the newfangled affectation of having footmen serve the guests with everything. She preferred the dishes to be left on the table and the guests to help themselves.

When the tepid pea soup had been drunk, she accordingly asked that the haunch of lamb be placed in front of Mr Garfield for that gentleman to carve.

Mice removed the silver cover from the dish. Mr Garfield picked up the carving knife and fork. Then his eyes narrowed and he gently poked at the

70

joint and turned it over. Someone appeared to have chewed a large mouthful out of the underside.

'I am afraid I cannot serve this, Lady Godolphin,' he said.

'Whyever not?' demanded Lady Godolphin, who was at the far end of the table, her view of the haunch being blocked by a silver épergne which depicted Wolfe scaling the heights of Quebec. It was an enormous épergne covered in nasty little silver figures doing quite awful things to each other.

'Because,' said Mr Garfield, putting down his knife and fork, 'someone has already been eating this.'

'Mice!' said Lady Godolphin awfully.

The butler laid his fat white head down on the sideboard behind Lady Godolphin and burst into tears. It was more than flesh and blood could stand, he moaned. He had been hired to buttle. He was not a kennel master. There were hell-hounds loose in the kitchens and the world was coming at an end.

'Pull yourself together,' snapped Lady Godolphin. 'I will speak to you later. Take away the haunch and serve the next course.'

Still weeping, the butler removed the haunch and snapped his fingers for his retinue of footmen to follow him.

Lady Godolphin mentally ticked off the dishes in the following course: harricot of mutton, breast of veal with stewed peas, raised pie *à la francaise*, fricassée of chicken, neck of venison, beef olives and sauce piquant, fish removed with rump of beef *à la Mantua.*

Daphne had been working up courage to ask Mr Garfield about Bellsire and Thunderer. She dreaded hearing that they had been flogged to

71

death or sold to another buyer or all sorts of horrible things. But he was talking to Lady Brothers who was seated on his other side. Daphne was not used to being ignored by any gentleman. She had never had to strain herself to think of anything interesting to say because the gentlemen seemed quite happy just to look at her. She was beginning to have a peculiar feeling that she had nothing at all to fear from the enigmatic Mr Garfield and that she bored him to tears.

The doors to the dining room swung open. Mice, much recovered, stood aside to let the retinue of footmen carrying heavy silver dishes file past.

Then an almost comical look of horror crossed his face and the first footman cast an anguished look of terror over his shoulder.

There was the sound of deep barking. The vicar's mouth fell open. There was the thud and scrabble of paws on the tiled floor of the hall and then shouts and curses from the footmen as they slid and staggered and then went down like ninepins amid an avalanche of hot dishes.

Bellsire and Thunderer erupted into the room.

Bellsire sniffed the air and launched himself at Mr Archer, who was seated near the vicar, getting the wrong quarry in his excitement.

Mr Archer glared in amazement at the mark of one large gravy-stained paw on his pantaloons, seized his table knife and tried to run Bellsire through the ribs.

'No you shall not!' screamed Daphne Armitage. She hurtled to her knees and grabbed wriggling armfuls of delighted dog.

'Who has been ill-treating these animals!' she cried, bosom heaving and eyes flashing.

The dogs licked her face. Her hair had tumbled down about her shoulders.

Mr Garfield's voice cut across the noise. 'I am afraid I am to blame,' he said. 'These are my hounds. They did not wish to leave my company, but rather than inflict them on your dinner party, my lady, I asked that they be confined to the kitchens.'

'Where they created terror and confusion,' sobbed Mice brokenly. 'Mr Garfield said we was not to tie them up and they were to be treated kind. They ran out the kitchen door fighting over that haunch of lamb.'

'Which you retrieved and nonetheless served up to the table,' pointed out Mr Garfield.

'What was I to do?' screamed the anguished butler to the gods. 'My lady would've have taken that haunch out of my wages.'

Daphne was muttering soothing things into the animals' floppy ears, occasionally flashing a glittering glance around the company as if daring anyone to harm a hair of their heads.

'Why aren't these dogs with Mr Apsley?' demanded Daphne.

'He turned out not to have a sympathetic approach to animals,' said Mr Garfield, admiring the quick rise and fall of Daphne's bosom. 'So I took it upon myself to rescue them.'

'Oh, that was *very* good of you,' said Daphne warmly. 'I would not have thought you to be so considerate.'

'I did it all for you, Miss Daphne,' mocked Mr Garfield.

Daphne quickly turned her head away.

'Here boys,' called the vicar and the dogs ran

73

up to him. 'Now sit!' he commanded. Bellsire and Thunderer lay quietly down at his feet.

'There you are,' said the vicar cheerfully. 'Well-trained beasts. The servants were probably teasing them something awful.'

'My dinner party is ruined,' said Lady Godolphin. 'The whole place smells of dog. Take them away. Take everything away. I'm ravished and there's nothing to eat.'

Daphne rose to her feet. 'Nonsense!' she said. 'I shall prepare you all something to eat. Mama will help me.'

'Daphne!' screamed that lady, clutching her heart. 'I could not. Every Sensibility would be affected. I feel a Spasm coming on.'

'Sit down, girl,' said Mrs Nash. 'You cannot go cavorting around the kitchens.'

'I am perfectly capable of cooking dinner,' said Daphne firmly.

'I've got a cook to do that,' pointed out Lady Godolphin.

'Cook's given notice,' said Mice with gloomy relish.

'On second thought,' smirked Mrs Nash, 'since Miss Armitage seems so determined to feed us, I suggest we let her try.'

'What do I care?' said Lady Godolphin. 'I've never seen such chassis in all my life. Take that mess away, Mice.'

The footmen were rapidly scooping up broken food back onto the dishes. Maids came in with mops and brushes. Daphne quietly left the room.

'Perhaps we should all go home,' suggested Lady Brothers.

'Fustian,' said Colonel Cartwright unexpectedly.

'I don't hold with this business of modern gels lettin' the servants do everything. In my day, a gently bred miss knew the kitchen and still room better than the housekeeper.'

'Can Daphne cook?' asked Lady Godolphin in an undertone to the vicar.

The vicar sadly shook his head. 'You know no one at the vicarage can cook, least of all Daphne. Pass around the wine and get 'em all in their altitudes. Then they won't notice. It's goodbye to Garfield.'

'I don't know,' muttered Lady Godolphin. 'If he took those dogs and made pets o' them, stands to reason he must have been trying to compress Daphne.'

An hour passed during which time the guests consumed a considerable amount of wine. Mrs Nash became quite flirtatious and kept rapping the vicar on the hand with the sticks of her fan.

Mr Archer was the only one apart from Mr Garfield who did not seem elated by the amount of wine. He was moodily bathing the stain on his pantaloons with soda water and salt.

Then the doors opened and two footmen came in bearing a huge raised pie.

It proved to contain a most peculiar mixture of viands, but the company were too hungry to care.

Only Mr Garfield had a shrewd suspicion that the enterprising Daphne had, he hoped, rinsed everything that had fallen on the floor under the tap, arranged it all in an enormous pie dish, and covered it with pastry. Certainly, it was the first time he had had fish, mutton, veal, chicken, neck of venison and beef olives all in the one dish.

When the third course appeared after another

hour, it was all too evident which dishes had been already prepared by the cook and which had been prepared by the fair Miss Daphne. The larded guinea fowl was slightly cold but quite delicious, as was the currant and raspberry pie which followed. But the omelette soufflé crouched at the bottom of the dish in a sullen mass and the macaroni was watery and half-cooked.

Daphne appeared, flushed with success, and got a warm round of applause.

The vicar, exalted by the admiring gleam he caught in Mr Garfield's eye, and being more tipsy than he had been since the last hunt, decided to honour the company with a song.

Raising his glass, he began in a rousing baritone:

'Come cheer up my lads! 'tis to glory we steer,
To add something more to this wonderful year;
To honour we call you, not press you like slaves,
For who are so free as the sons of the waves?'

Daphne, who had sat down beside Mr Garfield, half rose, red with embarrassment, already lifting a hand to try to silence her father. But Mr Garfield gently covered her hand with his own, and with an amused smile indicated the rest of the company who were already raising their glasses and roaring out the chorus:

'Heart of oak are our ships,
Heart of oak are our men:
We always are ready;
Steady, boys, steady;
We'll fight and we'll conquer again and again.'

76

It was then the turn of Lady Brothers who sang a mournful ballad in a tipsy voice:

'She is gone! Sweet Charlotte's gone,
Gone to the silent bourne;
She is gone, she's gone for ever more
She can never return.'

Lady Brothers subsided before a storm of enthusiastic applause and once more the wine bottles were circulated.

Colonel Cartwright promptly launched into a hunting song, much to the vicar's delight:

'Believer week is the bravest week
Of fifty-two in the year.
'Tis one to tweak a Methody's beak,
And to make a Teetotaler swear.
We leave our troubles and toils behind,
Forget if we've got grey hair
A parcel of boys, all frolic and noise,
Bidding begone dull care.'

Daphne gently pulled her hand away from under Mr Garfield's. It was making her feel hot and very odd. 'Is everyone drunk?' whispered Daphne to Mr Garfield.

'I do not know. I only know I am drunk by your beauty,' he said.

'I am disappointed in you, sir,' said Daphne now torn between attraction for him and the old longing to push him away. 'I thought you would have found something original to say.'

'I make the effort from time to time when I think

77

it will be appreciated. But why make the effort for you, Miss Daphne? By your taste,' he said, pointing with his quizzing glass to where Mr Archer sat gloomily looking at his knee, 'I would imagine you thrill to the sweet sound of the platitude, the cliché and the well-worn compliment.'

'You are rude.'

'Shh! Lady Godolphin is about to sing.'

Flushed in the face, swaying slightly and clutching a long pink chiffon scarf in her hands, Lady Godolphin was making weird sounds in her throat. Bellsire grumbled a warning under the table.

Lady Godolphin's noises grew stranger and her face grew redder and finally she opened her mouth and roared out a ballad at such volume it must have been heard all over the West End.

'Married women take advice,
Get you every thing that's nice,
A little drop of brandy, rum, or gin,
And if your husband should complain,
Give the compliment again,

And whack him with the wooden rolling pin.
When some women well-behaves,
They're oft used worse than slaves,
And must not dare to use their pretty tongue,
Let the world say what it will,
I will say, and prove it still,
That a woman never knows when her day's
    work's done.'

This was hailed with wild and noisy applause. But when Lord Brothers burst out with the opening lines of:

> 'A Captain bold, in Halifax, who dwelt in
>   country quarters,
> Seduced a maid who hang'd herself, one
>   morning in her garters.'

Mr Garfield arose and said he was establishing a new fashion by retiring *with* the ladies. He held out his arm to Daphne and led her from the room.

Rather subdued and beginning to feel the terrible effects of all they had drunk, not to mention Daphne's cooking, the guests trailed after them, each one beginning to say they had to go home.

Mr Garfield smiled down at Daphne. 'There is to be a Grand Review of Volunteers in Hyde Park tomorrow, Miss Daphne. May I ask your father if I may escort you?'

Daphne opened her mouth to refuse, but he suddenly smiled down into her eyes. Her knees trembled and she whispered very shyly, 'Yes.'

She turned away from him in confusion and caught a glimpse of her reflection in a long mirror. Her breasts stood out sharply against the thin muslin of her gown. She crossed her arms over her bosom and shivered slightly. What on earth had possessed her to wear such a shocking gown?

Mr Garfield was talking to her father who looked delighted. Mrs Armitage was looking pleased as well. Daphne felt a stab of irritation. Why should her mother—who had done absolutely nothing towards the upbringing of her daughters—suddenly interest herself in one of them for the first time? And why does it have to be me? thought Daphne crossly.

She was actually ashamed of her mother, a fact she would not even admit to herself. Mrs Armitage had never been told it is quite unsuitable for a short, plump woman to droop. She assumed all the languid die-away airs of a tall goddess.

Mr Garfield walked towards the door, Bellsire and Thunderer close at his heels. He looked down at them ruefully and then dug his hand in his pocket and slipped some coins into the butler's hand. Daphne could not see how much it was but Mice's face lit up like a sunrise and he actually bent and patted Bellsire on the head.

Mr Archer drew Daphne aside. 'Will you do me the honour of coming with me to Hyde Park tomorrow?' he asked, looking at his reflection in the glass over Daphne's shoulders.

'I cannot,' said Daphne impatiently. 'I *tried* to tell you. Papa wants me to marry Mr Garfield. Mr Garfield asked me to accompany him and I fear I accepted.'

Now for the first time that evening had she Mr Archer's full attention. 'But you must refuse,' he said simply.

'*I cannot.* I feel obliged to him for rescuing the dogs.'

'You did not even mention those wretched animals to me,' said Mr Archer with rare asperity. 'Had you done so, I would have done my utmost to find them for you.'

Daphne's gaze, which up till then had been a trifle hard, softened as it rested on Mr Archer's exquisite features. 'I should have told you,' she said. 'Do not worry. I shall contrive to give this Mr Garfield such a disgust of me on the morrow

80

that he will not want to see me again.' She looked around quickly. Her father and mother were talking earnestly to Lady Godolphin. The other guests had left.

'Do you really love me and want to marry me?' whispered Daphne.

'Very much,' said Mr Archer, taking her hand in his and giving it a warm press.

'Hey, what's this?' cried the vicar, blustering up. 'Come along, Daphne. Goodbye Mr Archer. I have no doubt we shall *not* be seeing much of you in the future.'

Cyril Archer looked at the little vicar with hauteur. Daphne hurried to leave with her parents before her father could say any more.

Outside the house, Hanover Square felt soupy and suffocatingly hot.

'We'll soon be able to go home to the country,' yawned the vicar sleepily when they were all settled in the carriage. 'Thank goodness the harvest is in. I smell rain.'

'How you can smell anything other than drains is a miracle,' said Mrs Armitage. 'I was proud of you tonight, Daphne. All my daughters married well. What a triumph.'

'I am *not* going to marry Mr Garfield,' said Daphne between clenched teeth.

But her parents had paid no attention to any of her remarks in the past and so they paid no attention now. Daphne had always been such a good, biddable sort of girl.

She would do what she was told.

CHAPTER FOUR

The next day dawned brassy and sultry. Daphne felt she would never feel fresh or clean again. Mrs Armitage had announced her intention of calling on Annabelle before Daphne left for the Review. The maid, Betty, was to accompany them.

Daphne felt depressed as Betty helped her into a sprigged muslin gown. The normally cheerful Betty was sour and sullen.

'What is the matter, Betty?' asked Daphne. 'Have we done something to offend you? You should say so, you know, and not keep tugging my hair and wrenching at the tapes of my gown to show your disapproval.'

'I have the headache and I don't want for to go to Miss Annabelle's, I mean Lady Brabington.' And with that, Betty sat down, threw her apron over her head, and burst into tears.

'Are you sure it is just the headache?' asked Daphne anxiously.

'Ye-es,' sobbed the maid, crying harder than ever.

Daphne gently lowered the apron and dabbed at Betty's streaming face with a handkerchief. 'You did not marry your John,' she said softly. 'Is this what ails you?'

But Betty would only rock from side to side and cry harder.

'Let me help you to your room,' said Daphne, now really worried. Despite Betty's protests, she summoned two of the housemaids. Still weeping, Betty was helped to her room and made to undress and go to bed. Tea was brought to her and Daphne sat beside the bed, holding Betty's hand, occasionally smoothing the tumbled black curls from the maid's hot brow, until worn out with crying, Betty fell asleep.

Mrs Armitage was fretting downstairs. Why had Daphne taken such an unconscionable time to get ready? Mr Garfield was to call for her at Annabelle's. She, Mrs Armitage, had despatched a footman requesting him to do so.

In that way, they would have plenty of time for a comfortable cose with Annabelle.

Daphne wished all of a sudden that Deidre would return from Brighton. Deirdre was always bright and merry and so much in love with her handsome husband. And why hadn't Annabelle gone to Brighton? It seemed silly to stay in London in all this suffocating heat when one did not have to.

Endless articles were written in the newspapers about the strangely hot summer. There had been just such a summer fifteen years before but everyone went on as if the end of the world was at hand.

When they arrived at Conduit Street it was to find the Marquess of Brabington's travelling carriage drawn up outside the door and trunks being loaded onto the back.

'Annabelle must be leaving for the country,' exclaimed Mrs Armitage. 'She has quite forgot to tell us.'

The Marquess of Brabington's tall figure appeared on the steps. He swept off his hat as Daphne and Mrs Armitage descended from their carriage.

'You will find my wife in the drawing room,' he said. 'I regret I cannot wait to speak to you. I am leaving for Brabington Court. The estates have been sadly neglected of late.'

'Annabelle goes with you?' asked Mrs Armitage, a trifle flustered by the stern look on the marquess's face.

'No, she is content to remain in town,' he said coldly. 'Now, if you will excuse me . . .'

He walked past them and climbed into the carriage.

Daphne remembered the days shortly after Annabelle's wedding when the Marquess of Brabington had seemed the happiest man in London. She and Mrs Armitage watched in silence as the marquess's carriage drove off and then they entered the tall dark house.

They could hear the lusty wailing of the baby coming from the drawing room.

Annabelle looked quite unlike her usual beautiful and frivolous self. Her blonde hair was lank and her face had grown thin. She was walking up and down, rocking the screaming child, while the nanny, Mrs Arbuckle, made ineffectual efforts to remove the baby from her.

Daphne thought uncomfortably that baby Charles was the sort of child only a mother could love. When his face was not red with crying, it was dark with rage. She could never remember having seen a small baby with such a low brow. He had a thatch of thick wiry black hair and large chubby fists with which he was engaged at that moment in punching his mother's face.

'Oh, there you are,' sighed Annabelle, admitting defeat and passing the boy to Mrs Arbuckle who

84

carried him swiftly from the room.

Perhaps it was because the baby had seemed to arrive with so little warning and because one had had so little time to get used to the idea of Annabelle being a mother that had made little Charles seem such a ferocious cuckoo in the Brabington nest.

Annabelle had retired to the country for six months before the arrival of the baby, which certainly all went to show she was determined to bring a healthy child into the world, for nothing else could have persuaded Annabelle to be away from fashionable London for so long. She had led a very quiet life, refusing even to see Minerva. She had written regularly to all her sisters, only announcing two months before the birth that the baby was expected.

Daphne chided herself for having such nasty thoughts about this newest nephew and smiled at her sister.

'Is not this weather frightful? I am like a wet rag,' said Annabelle, plumping herself down inelegantly in a chair. 'Do sit down Mother. Daphne, ring for the tea tray.'

Daphne tugged at the bellrope and Annabelle studied her sister's beautiful face, modish gown, and artistically arranged hair

'Faith,' sighed Annabelle, 'to think I was once the beauty of the family. You were always well enough, Daphne, but no one could have guessed you would blossom into a diamond of the first water.'

'Mr Simon Garfield is to call here to take her to the Review in Hyde Park,' said Mrs Armitage proudly.

Annabelle's blue eyes gleamed with amusement. 'Mr Garfield. The *very* rich Corinthian Mr Garfield! Papa will be in alt. Except I have heard that Mr Garfield excels at all sports *except* fox-hunting.'

'Annabelle,' said Daphne anxiously. 'Brabington was just leaving when we arrived. He is gone to the country.'

'I know *that*, you silly goose.'

Tut . . . but I find it strange that you are not going with him.'

Annabelle gave a shrill laugh. 'I was like you once, Daphne, all wrapped around with the gold tissue of love's young dream. Mr Garfield must have captured your heart.'

'No, Annabelle. I am almost affianced to Mr Archer.'

'Cyril Archer? Oh, Daphne, how boring! Now Mr Garfield looks a very exciting sort of man.'

'I don't *want* to be excited,' said Daphne crossly.

'Ah, we'll see,' grinned Annabelle, and then her grin faded to be replaced by a look of pain. 'Make the very best of it,' she shrugged. 'Nothing lasts.'

Daphne looked at Mrs Armitage for help. Surely that lady could see Annabelle and her husband must have had the most terrible kind of row. But Mrs Armitage began to talk dreamily about Mr Garfield's perfections until even Annabelle became irritated and asked her mother tartly whether she did not wish to marry Mr Garfield herself.

The arrival of the tea tray saved Mrs Armitage from replying.

Searching in her mind for a safe topic of conversation Daphne told Annabelle about Betty's distress.

'I am sure it is not the headache, you know,'

86

Daphne finished earnestly.

'I am sure there is some trouble between Betty and John Summer. They were to be married but nothing came of it. Papa must be paying John a fair wage because his livery is very fine but . .

'This heat,' interrupted Annabelle acidly, 'is quite bad enough without having to listen to gossip about servants.'

Daphne's beautiful mouth folded into a stern line. 'What has come over you, Bella?' she said severely. 'When did we refer to Betty and John Summer as *servants* in that tone of voice? Only mushrooms and counter-jumpers talk of their servants so.'

'Oh, Miss Hoity-Toity with your newfound London airs,' sneered Annabelle.

'Girls! Girls!' cried Mrs Armitage feebly. 'You will bring on one of my Spasms. And Daphne, I have observed since last night that your face has started to *move* a great deal. You will bring on premature wrinkles.'

'Ah, yes,' said Annabelle maliciously, 'what has happened to our dim little sphinx-like Daphne? You are become positively human and your nose is quite shiny. Has Mr Garfield kissed the sleeping princess to life?'

'You are sadly gone off in looks, Bella,' said Daphne coldly, 'which is no doubt why you are become such a jealous *cat*.'

'Do not let us quarrel,' sighed Annabelle, going suddenly limp. She pushed a fretful hand at the heavy mass of her hair. 'I do not know what I am about these days. I say such terrible things to Peter, but. I can't help it. He cannot even bear to look at his own son! It . . . it's *unnatural*.'

There was an awkward silence, and then Annabelle shrugged and started to gossip about clothes and notables. Daphne could not help glancing every now and then towards the clock. The air in the dark drawing room was oppressive.

Why had Annabelle not tried to redecorate? There must be thunder about. Daphne glanced again at the clock. She felt a suffocating feeling of anticipation in her bosom. If only Mr Garfield would arrive so that she might get it over with and return to the calm tenor of her ways. She did not want to see Mr Garfield although he had been most kind about the dogs. He was too upsetting. The hands of the clock which had seemed to crawl around the face suddenly leapt forward and the clock struck four.

As the last chime died away, there came a rap at the street door. Mrs Armitage leapt to the looking glass with quite amazing alacrity and began to arrange her straw hat at a more becoming angle. Daphne nervously straightened her gown, and Annabelle watched them both with wide, cynical eyes.

'Mr Garfield.'

Annabelle's hand flew to her hair. Daphne blushed and Mrs Armitage simpered.

'Welcome, Mr Garfield,' said Annabelle. 'So you are come to take my little sister out. Do have a care. These country misses have not yet acquired our town bronze and become alarmed in crowds.'

'I have never seen Miss Daphne other than very poised and very beautiful,' said Mr Garfield.

'You must see my darling son,' cried Annabelle, jumping to her feet. As she caught a glimpse of herself in the looking glass over the fireplace a look

88

of dismay crossed her features, and she hurriedly whipped herself out of the room.

'I am sure the Review will be a splendid sight,' sighed Mrs Armitage. 'I had so hoped to see it but Mr Armitage *did* insist on going to his club and there is no gentleman to escort me.'

She cast a roguish look out of her faded eyes at Mr Garfield but Mr Garfield seemed vastly interested in the polished toes of his boots.

'How go Bellsire and Thunderer?' asked Daphne desperately.

She felt she had wandered into a strange dream where she sat in a darkened room talking to a man with yellow eyes while her normally beautiful sister behaved like a shrew and her normally indifferent mother began to show alarming symptoms of rivalling Lady Godolphin in the arts of middle-aged flirtation.

'They consented to let me go,' he smiled. 'They really are hunting dogs, you know, Miss Daphne, and quite unsuitable for a gentleman's residence. I am persuaded your father would be delighted to have them back again.'

'Oh, I am sure he would,' said Daphne eagerly. Then she strove to put her usual calm mask on but somehow she could not achieve it. Every part of her felt alive and tingling.

The door opened and a refurbished and beautiful Annabelle appeared wearing a saucy pink silk gown with many ribbons.

'Alas!' she cried. 'Little Charles is sleeping like an angel and I dare not wake him.'

'I shall no doubt have the pleasure of seeing your son another time, Lady Brabington,' said Mr Garfield. 'And now if you are ready, Miss

Daphne . . .?'

'You are leaving so soon?' said Annabelle, waving a pretty fan and flirting with her large blue eyes over the top of it. 'It is so hot here, I *pine* for fresh air. I am sure the air of Hyde Park would be very beneficial.'

'On the contrary, I fear it is about to rain,' smiled Mr Garfield. 'But Miss Daphne is still countrified enough to stand the rigours of inclement weather, so, in that, I am fortunate. Your husband will no doubt return soon . . .'

'Lud! Brabington's gone this day to the country.'

'Then you should follow him,' said Mr Garfield, picking up Daphne's parasol and stole. 'The air would do you and your child the world of good.' He swept Daphne rather hurriedly from the room. 'I have decided it would be best to walk,' said Mr Garfield when they had left the house.

Daphne took his offered arm. She wondered whether to apologize for her mother and her sister's odd behaviour. They had practically thrown themselves at Mr Garfield's head!

The air was very still and humid beneath a sky which seemed to be darkening by the minute.

Mr Garfield's broad shoulders pushed through the crowd and secured them a place at the front.

Coloured flags hung limply between the trees and a hot-looking band were playing hot-sounding military marches.

Then the drums began to beat to arms from every quarter summoning the reviewers and the reviewed to the field.

The avenues of the park were crowded with elegantly dressed women escorted by their beaux. The crowd was so great that when the Prince of

Wales entered the park, it was thought advisable to lock the gates to avoid too much pressure.

Colours stood out very sharply in the close, darkening scene. There were uniforms of every hue. The Honourable and Ancient Artillery Company wore blue with scarlet and gold facings, pipe-clayed belts and black gaiters. The Bloomsbury and Inns of Court Volunteers were dressed in scarlet with yellow facings, white waistcoats and black gaiters. The Volunteer Rifles were clad in green.

Daphne was thrilled by her first sight of the Prince of Wales. To others he might appear gross, but to Daphne every inch of his corpulent form looked royal.

The Volunteers were a useful body. They served as police, and were duly drummed to church on National Fast and Thanksgiving days to represent the national party. The strength of the Volunteers had been at its peak over ten years ago when everyone had dreaded an invasion by Bonaparte.

Although now not so great in number, they were still very popular with the highest to the lowest since every man had a wish to be with the colours, an enthusiasm shared by the Prince Regent who had many times longed to go into action and who had so many times been refused permission. A large warm drop of rain plopped down on Daphne's nose and she looked anxiously up at the sky. The clouds were dark purple, so heavy they seemed to lie on top of the trees. Near at hand, the thunder growled.

There was a great blinding flash. Faces stood out white, colours sharp and brilliant, and the blackness swept over the Park as the rain came down with a great torrential burst.

There was no possibility of fleeing from the Park. The gates were locked and the Prince Regent was still reviewing the troops. Mr Garfield took Daphne's parasol and held it over both their heads. Slowly the glory of the troops began to fade as their splendid uniforms lost all their gloss.

The smoke of a whole campaign could not have more discoloured them. Where the ground was hard, they slipped; where soft, they sank up to the knee. The water ran out of their cuffs as from a spout and filled up their half boots so that they squished and squashed with every step.

Water was beginning to run down the handle of the parasol and drip through the thin silk onto Daphne's head. Her smart straw bonnet was becoming limp, her feet in their yellow silk sandals were beginning to sink into the quagmire that was forming at her feet.

Worse than that, many of their neighbours were beginning to crush in close to try to share some of the parasol and Daphne was rammed up hard against Mr Garfield. It was *indecent*, thought Daphne, that a muslin gown should offer so little protection. She might as well have been naked. She was conscious of every hard muscle in Mr Garfield's tall hard body. She tried to inch away from him, but found she could not. She squirmed uncomfortably against him and that seemed to make matters worse.

In despair, she twisted about and found herself bosom to chest with a fat, florid man with a wicked gleam in his eye, and so she wriggled back around again.

'Better the evil you know . . .' murmured Mr Garfield's voice somewhere above her

Drowned, sodden and battered, the flower of London society stood stoically while sheets of rain poured down, the thunder bellowed and the lightning flashed.

At long last, after two hours, the Prince Regent's carriage moved off and the gates of the park were unlocked.

Mr Garfield held Daphne back as she tried to make a frenzied dash through the crowd.

'We are so very wet,' he said ruefully, throwing away the remains of her parasol, 'that it will not hurt us to get a little wetter. We will be trampled underfoot by the mob if we try to leave now.'

He led her over to the shelter of a large oak. Daphne dragged her thin gauze stole about her shoulders.

Never before had she been so conscious of her body. Never before had she shown so much of it in public. Her wet dress was clinging to every inch of her form. The straw brim of her hat sagged over her eyes. She impatiently undid the ribbons and let her hat fall to the ground.

Mr Garfield pulled off his coat and put it about her shoulders. He was smiling down at her in a way that was making her breathless and frightened.

'Oh, do let us go,' she said, feeling she could not bear it any longer.

She set off across the quagmire of the Park.

And then, through the pounding rain, she thought she saw the elegant figure of Mr Archer. He was walking towards the gate, carrying a large umbrella.

Sanctuary. Safe Mr Archer. Dull, unimaginative Mr Archer who never frightened her or did all these strange things to her body.

Daphne heard Mr Garfield call out behind her but paid no heed.

She plunged towards the retreating figure of the man with the umbrella. The next minute she had sunk up to her garters in the mud. She floundered to extricate herself. Mr Garfield came up behind her and put a strong arm about her waist to help her. But the emotions roused by the feel of that hard muscled arm under the softness of her bosom made Daphne struggle so wildly and so violently that they both fell over in the mud.

Mr Garfield lay full length on the ground beside Daphne, propped his head up on one hand and surveyed her wide, startled, terrified eyes with amusement.

'Fair Daphne,' he said. 'Only you, out of all the ladies I know, could still appear exquisite when covered with mud.' Still laughing, he pulled her into his arms and kissed her, seemingly oblivious of the thundering rain and the muddy ground. For one brief moment all that held her to the world was his lips against hers. And then Daphne became alive to her situation. She had involuntarily wound her arms about his neck. They were both lying in the mud, and a passing lady stared down at them and let out a hysterical giggle.

'Help me up, Mr Garfield,' said Daphne icily. 'I am like to catch my death of cold.'

He got to his feet and pulled her up and then lifted her up into his arms clear of the mud and started to walk off with her towards the gate.

'Put me down,' said Daphne weakly.

'When we reach dry ground.'

'You should not have kissed me.'

'The temptation was too great. You should not

94

have fallen in the mud. You looked so deliciously abandoned.'

'Sir, you must remember I am almost affianced to Mr Archer.'

'Indeed? Does he kiss you like this . . . and this . . . and this . . .?'

'Oh, Mr Garfield. You should not. Put me down. Oh, Mr *Garfield.*'

At last he raised his lips from hers and smiled down at her worried, startled face.

'I shall tell my father,' whispered Daphne.

'Who would be delighted.'

'No, he would not,' said Daphne regaining her composure as they reached the gates of the Park and he set her down. 'He would be most shocked that a gentleman should subject me to . . . to . . .'

'To such an excess of civility.'

'To such *humiliation.* Such familiarities, sir, should be between married people.'

Mr Garfield looked down at her in surprise. He took her arm and tucked it in his, and led the way along the glistening pavement. He had just realized that he had been guilty of quite dreadful behaviour. Unless he meant to marry her, then he had better apologize and try to convince her he was foxed. If she did tell her father, then the good vicar would soon be appearing with the marriage service in one hand and a gun in the other.

'I am truly sorry,' he said abruptly. 'I did not mean to subject you to such behaviour. I had rather too much wine at luncheon and that combined with the sight of your beauty went to my head. Please forgive me and forget the whole distasteful episode. Come! Smile at me Daphne. I will dance at your wedding to Mr Archer.'

Daphne smiled weakly and mumbled that she forgave him. She felt very depressed and miserable and cold. She wanted to lie down at home in bed and pull the covers over her head and never, ever emerge until it was time to return to Hopeworth. Covered in rivulets of mud though they were, both had now become very chilly and formal.

So he took her home and left her on the step, bowing very stiffly to her before striding off into the rain.

Daphne went slowly into the house.

It was only when she got to her room that she realized she still had his jacket about her shoulders.

*　　*　　*

The Reverend Charles Armitage was a very depressed man. He had had high hopes of Mr Garfield. His wife had told him that a marriage with Daphne was definitely on the cards. And now the dratted man was nowhere to be found.

A week had passed since that day in the Park, the Armitage family had trotted Daphne to every event that off-Season London had to offer, but although Mr Archer seemed to be everywhere, Mr Garfield was not.

Daphne appeared perfectly comfortable with Mr Archer and had returned to her old glass-faced perfection. At long last the vicar remembered his prayer and decided to give Daphne his blessing.

The harvest had been excellent. He was comfortably off. If Mr Archer was what Daphne wanted, then Daphne should have him. Mr Armitage did not like Mr Archer, but, nonetheless, considered him harmless. Perhaps if Squire

Radford had been present, he might have advised the vicar to wait until the following year. But the vicar, although mercenary, had always a very guilty conscience about this his main character defect, and letting Daphne marry whom she pleased seemed a splendid way of placating that very terrible God Who sat in the clouds somewhere above the vicar's head.

There was only a very thin coating of civilization over the vicar's primitive soul, and so deep down he believed—when he believed in anything—in a God of wrath who needed burnt offerings and sacrifices: at times the vicar considered Him a very odd God indeed, since He did not seem in the least to appreciate the periodic offering up of various dead foxes.

Accordingly, as a week without Mr Garfield moved into yet another week without any sign of that gentleman, the vicar sent for Daphne and told that very surprised young lady that she might feel free to name the day any time she chose.

Then he sat and watched Daphne's face, reflecting it had never looked so beautiful or so blank.

Daphne had received a shock. A Mr Archer who was forbidden fruit held all sorts of exciting charms. A Mr Archer who was accepted by the family was another matter. On the other hand, Mr Simon Garfield had kissed and run.

Mr Garfield was insultingly absent. Daphne had heard several *on dits* about Mr Garfield. It seemed he was a confirmed bachelor but that had not stopped 'several silly misses from quite breaking their hearts over him'. Therefore an engagement to Mr Archer would show that chilly man that he had meant nothing to her. Which was *true*, thought Daphne savagely. On the other hand, if she married Mr Archer then she would never have a Season with all its balls and parties and pretty gowns. She would be an old married woman, sitting in the chimney corner, listening to her husband digress intelligently on the best way to remove wine stains from silk.

Aloud Daphne said, 'Thank you, Papa. Mama and Annabelle will be quite cast down. They quite pined to see me wed Mr Garfield.'

'Unlike them to take an interest,' pointed out the vicar.

'Well, if you cannot wed someone yourself, the next best thing is to get him in the family,' said Daphne with rare malice. 'Mama was so outrageous, I had fears of you calling on Mr Garfield and challenging him to a duel.'

'What!' The startled anger on the vicar's face quickly fled before an enormous grin. 'Wicked puss. Your mama has never looked at any man with interest in the whole of her born life—and that includes me.'

'Oh, it had to be seen to be believed,' said Daphne sweetly, 'and Annabelle all but came out and begged him to take her to the Park too. Of course, Mama had just tried the same thing, but Annabelle is another matter. She is still young, although some people think twenty-one is fast approaching middle-age, and she has gone off in looks, so to see her making a cake of herself over another man was quite sad.'

Daphne lowered her eyelashes and pleated a fold of her skirt.

The vicar studied his beautiful daughter intently.

98

'Never knew you to tell fibs before, Daphne. Annabelle's in love with that husband of hers. She's got a new baby ...'

'She dotes on *the baby.*' Daphne's better self rose above her unrecognized jealousy and she said impulsively, 'Oh, Papa, Annabelle is so very unhappy, and Brabington too. Something is badly wrong. Pray go and see her.'

'I will, I will,' said the vicar. 'Hey, you ain't thanked me.'

'For what?'

'For saying you can marry that caper-merchant, Archer.'

'Why are you so anxious to marry me off if you do not like the gentleman? It's not as if he is rich.'

'Women!' groaned the vicar. 'Well, if you don't want him, stop encouraging him.'

'But I do want him!'

'Don't sound like it to me,' said Mr Armitage, becoming suddenly suspicious. 'Nothing to do with Garfield, I trust?'

'Of course not!'

'There's a story going round the clubs about the day of the Review. Seems some member of the *ton* was lying in the mud kissing some young miss. You came home covered in mud. Wasn't you by any chance?'

'Papa!'

'No, I thought not.'

The door opened and the butler came in with the post. The vicar idly ruffled through the letters and cards. 'Here's one from Minerva.' He broke open the seal and scanned the contents. 'Seems she is staying on in Brighton. Deirdre and Harry have taken off for France. *France!* Pah. What's in France you can't get in England?'

'Good cooking and good clothes.'

'Don't be impertinent. Let's see what else she says. Baby Julian is well. Peregrine and James are well. Mmm. Oh, she wonders if you would like to join her for a few days before returning to Hopeworth.'

Daphne thought of escaping from London. No more listening to Mr Archer worrying about the set of his cravat, no more entering some salon half-dreading, half-hoping the irritating Mr Garfield would be there.

'I should like to go very much.'

'I'll speak to Mrs Armitage. Be off with you. I'll call on Annabelle and see what I can do.'

*   *   *

The vicar was relieved to find Annabelle very much restored to her former beauty although her face was a trifle too thin and there were shadows under her eyes. He was irritated to find Mr Archer very much present in Annabelle's drawing room. Annabelle had always been a flirt, reflected the vicar sourly, but she was going much too far with Mr Archer.

The vicar turned a fulminating gaze on that exquisite young man.

'See here,' he growled, 'I want to have a word in private with my daughter, so . . .'

'But I am come to take Lady Brabington driving!'

'Got the wrong daughter, haven't you?'

'Mr Armitage, Daphne's sisters are as dear to me as she is herself.'

'*Miss* Daphne to you,' snapped the vicar. 'Oh, very well. Be a good chap and wait in your carriage.'

Mr Archer gave a magnificent leg and sauntered out.

'What are you up to?' asked the vicar.

Annabelle fanned herself. 'Nothing,' she said airily. 'I am bored, that is all, and I find Mr Archer a most undemanding young man.'

Mr Archer, standing in the hall, pulling on his gloves, heard the sound of his own name and decided to eavesdrop:

'I told Daphne she could marry him if she wants,' he heard the vicar say. Mr Archer smiled complaisantly. Annabelle's reply was indistinct.

'Strange,' came the vicar's voice again, 'for I could have sworn she was slightly taken with Garfield. Now, what's this I hear about you? Daphne would have it you were making sheep's eyes at Garfield.'

'Jealous cat,' said Annabelle. 'It was quite the other way around. Mr Garfield could not take his eyes off *me*. You know how gentlemen are, Papa.'

'You're well enough, I grant you that,' said the vicar brutally, 'but no man in his right mind is going to look at a married woman with a squalling baby when there's a diamond of the first water like Daphne in the same room.'

'I am accounted the beauty of the family,' said Annabelle.

'Yes, but that was before Daphne began to outshine you. Never mind all this. What I want to know is why you and Brabington have quarrelled and why you are so unhappy.'

'It's a silly marital squabble,' said Annabelle. 'I am unhappy because I am bored.'

'*You* are bored!' the vicar's angry voice came quite clearly through the door panels to Mr

101

Archer's listening ears. 'You are a spoilt brat and I wish you would tell the truth. I *know* what ails Brabington. It's because I was able to give you a child and he cannot! So you'll just need to talk him round.'

Mr Archer stood very still, his eyes wide with shock. Then he quickly scampered from the house and sat in his carriage his heart beating hard. Here was startling news!

Incest!

London would have heard nothing like it since the Byron scandal.

Mr Archer forced himself to relax. This piece of information could prove useful. He was anxious to wed Daphne Armitage because he sensed in her a sexual coldness and purity which appealed to him vastly. The Armitage family had become famous in society by virtue of Daphne's elder three sisters' dazzling marriages. Daphne's brothers-in-law were all very rich men. Although Daphne could not be expected to bring any very great dowry to the marriage, she was well enough connected to ensure that Mr Archer could spend a long life of ease, staying with his various in-laws. Mr Archer did not want children. He certainly did not want to go about begetting them. But there were still some rumours circulating about London which he wished to quash and this he could do by marrying Daphne Armitage. It was important to secure Daphne before she made her come-out when the competition would be fierce.

In Daphne, he would have a beautiful piece of porcelain for a wife. Recently, when Simon Garfield had appeared on the scene, he had been afraid that Daphne might turn out as other women,

102

but then Mr Garfield had disappeared and Daphne was once more her usual, beautiful, calm, aloof self.

No other woman would do. No other woman would fit the bill so exactly. But Mr Archer saw a few rocks and shoals ahead. Now he had this fascinating bit of gossip which would ruin the Armitages for life.

He would hug it close and use it carefully if the necessity arose.

The door opened and Annabelle came out. She was much flushed. Her squat and burly father stood glowering on the doorstep. Mr Archer allowed himself a delicate shudder. How could Lady Brabington possibly . . .?

And *he* had once been called decadent!

His beautiful mouth curved in its classical smile and he set himself out to be as charming as possible to Annabelle.

He had always been somewhat afraid of the vicar but now he felt a glorious sensation of power. He waved cheerfully to Mr Armitage and set his team in motion.

Annabelle's better self had taken over. She was feeling guilty, she was missing her husband badly, and the only thing she found to comfort her was Mr Archer's infectious high spirits.

He must be in love, thought Annabelle. Perhaps Daphne has made a wise choice.

*   *   *

Mrs Armitage appeared to have lost all her interest in Daphne's affairs. After seeming very cast down at the news that Daphne was to marry Mr Archer, Mrs Armitage had once more resorted to her patent medicines and her bed.

On hearing that Daphne was to set out for Brighton, Diana and Frederica begged to be allowed to return to Hopeworth and Mrs Armitage said faintly she would be glad to return to the country. Mr Armitage could escort Daphne if he wished and the maid, Betty, could go also.

Daphne was glad to escape London. The weather was once more hot and close. As the carriage bowled through the early morning streets she could not help glancing out, just to see if there might be a glimpse of a tall man with copper hair and two foxhounds.

The air of Brighton was bracing and the sea was as blue as the almost-forgotten Mr Archer's eyes.

Brighton had been discovered by the young Prince of Wales in 1783 when he had been told to try sea-bathing to cure the swollen glands in his neck. He bought a farmhouse and set about redesigning it. The final result was the Pavilion, the splendour of its rooms making even the jewelled splendour of his guests' clothes appear insignificant. It was one of the wonders of the age, its walls decorated with mandarins and fluted yellow draperies to resemble the tents of the Chinese, its peach-blossom ceilings and canopies of tassels and bells, its imperial five-clawed dragons darting from every chandelier and over-mantel.

Daphne thought it a fairy palace and wondered at the scorn of the critics. One wrote:

. . . A China view
Where neither genius, taste, nor fancy dwells:
Monkeys, mandarins, a motley crew,
Bridges, pagodas, swings, and tinkling bells.

104

And that wit, Sydney Smith, had said acidly, it looked 'as if St Paul's had gone to the sea and pupped'.

Its domes sparkled in the sunlight as the Reverend Armitage drove his daughter past, enjoying her awe. Although the vicar outwardly joined the fashionable in condemning the Pavilion, he privately thought it 'a deuced fine show' and, in truth, secretly considered most things regarded as good taste as deadly dull.

Daphne was a most rewarding audience. She found her first view of the ocean thrilling in the extreme. Her eyes travelled from the stately houses glittering with fresh paint in the sunlight to the colourful ranks of bathing boxes on the long line of rock and shingle.

Everything seemed to flutter and dance in the bright light, from the skirts of the ladies' muslin gowns to the sails of the yachts bobbing on that incredible expanse of blue water.

The pier with its wooden deck balanced on ranks of elegant slender piles had the spindly elegance of a heron, treading delicately out to sea.

The very air was an aphrodisiac, although Daphne did not understand this, and therefore did not understand why Mr Garfield's hard face seemed to rise up in her mind to blot out the bright scene.

She was not all that far removed from the schoolroom, and, very much like a child, she begged her father, 'Oh, please. Will I be able to bathe?'

'Of course,' said the vicar indulgently. 'Might have a go myself.' He was glad the male bathers were far enough removed from his daughter's wide innocent gaze, however, since no man in his right mind wore anything at all when going for a swim, unlike the ladies who had to be covered from head to foot in flannel.

Minerva's house faced the sea, a tall white building with green shutters and black iron balconies.

It was a relief to Daphne to find Minerva much the same as ever. She and her husband appeared to be very much in love and Minerva confided shyly she was expecting her second child.

Julian was a chubby, sturdy little boy, extremely good-natured. He adored his young uncles, the twins Peregrine and James, who dropped their newly acquired lordly manners and rolled about the floor entertaining Julian and behaving very much like the schoolboys that they were.

There was something so bright and cheerful and *normal* about Minerva's household that Daphne felt all her worries begin to fade. It was like being a child again with Minerva on hand to fuss and lecture. The old moralizing Minerva had largely gone although enough of her original character remained to make her appear a safe rock in a sea of frivolous fashion.

When Daphne's things were unpacked, Minerva was delighted to find an excuse to give her beloved son an airing and agreed to Daphne's suggestion that they should go for a walk. Little Julian was tucked up in his small carriage, his eyes, large and green and unwavering like his father's, placidly surveying the summer scene.

Daphne attracted a good deal of attention from the strolling bucks and bloods. 'We will have you married before you even leave Brighton,' teased

Minerva.

'I have already found the man I am going to marry,' said Daphne, wondering why as she said it the summer scene seemed to lose a lot of its sparkle.

Minerva eagerly began to ply her sister with questions, becoming increasingly anxious over Daphne's very evident lack of enthusiasm.

'Daphne, dear,' said Minerva hesitatingly. 'Papa is often a great deal too managing. You must not let him thrust you into a marriage you do not want. If it all becomes too much for you, then you may make your home with me.'

'Oh, I want to marry Mr Archer,' said Daphne in a dreary little voice. 'Papa was quite against the match but then he changed his mind.'

'Perhaps you are fatigued after your journey?' suggested Minerva. 'You do not seem at all excited by the prospect of your engagement. Perhaps you should wait until you have had your Season. You are very young and cannot have met very many eligible men.'

'I do not think Mr Archer wishes to wait that long.'

'I am not surprised,' said Minerva drily. 'You are a very attractive girl and he must know you will command a lot of attention when you make your come-out. Also, it is not just a question of Papa's approval. Sylvester and your other brothers-in-law have promised to add considerably to your dowry, and they will all naturally expect to approve of your future husband.'

'Very well,' said Daphne meekly.

Minerva glanced at her younger sister with sur prise mixed with amusement. 'Do not tell me Papa has at last found a meek and biddable daughter.'

'Oh, I will always do as Papa wishes,' said Daphne, looking vaguely out to sea. 'Enough of my affairs,' she said, turning again to her sister, a frown of worry between her brows. 'Things do not go well with Annabelle.'

Minerva sighed. 'Annabelle often appears flighty and sometimes she says hard things, but underneath she is a fine, warm-hearted girl. She also loves her husband very much.'

'She loves her baby more,' said Daphne. 'And such a baby! I do not wish to be cruel, but he is such an angry, exhausting, ugly child. Brabington has been quite driven away from home, and, oh!, Minerva, worse than that, Annabelle went so far as to flirt openly with one of my beaux.'

'Well, Annabelle is apt to *appear* to flirt and . . .'

'No. She was quite blatant, and Mama too. I was never more shocked.'

'Mama! You must be funning. No, I see you are not. Who is this paragon of male beauty who has caused such a flutter?'

'Garfield. Mr Simon Garfield.'

'I have only seen Mr Garfield once, and very briefly. He has a highly fashionable reputation but does not go about in society much. He seems to prefer the company of his own sex to the exclusion of ours. I cannot remember him as appearing much out of the common way,' said Minerva who really thought any man other than her husband quite uninteresting.

'He is rather overbearing and autocratic,' said Daphne. 'But he is most kind to animals and *that* must always be a redeeming feature.'

108

'Never say he leapt in front of Papa's horse and saved the fox.'

'Nothing like that,' grinned Daphne. She told Minerva the story of Bellsire and Thunderer. Much emboldened by Minerva's appreciation of the story, Daphne went on to tell Minerva about the day of the Review.

Minerva's amusement fled and she came to a sudden halt. 'This will never do,' she said severely. 'You must take pains to avoid this Mr Garfield, no matter what. It was fortunate that the weather was so inclement that society had not time to stop and stare. My dear girl. Your reputation could have been in ruins! No man makes such outrageous advances to a lady. If you had said he had pressed your hand, I would have considered he had gone too far. Your morals shock me! Did you not scream and shout for help?'

Daphne blushed and shook her head.

Minerva opened her mouth to lecture further when she suddenly remembered one of her first encounters with her husband. She had leapt into his bed at the inn at Hopeminster. Certainly, she had been under the impression it was her own room and her own bed, but still . . . Then Minerva straightened her spine. But *never* would she have rolled around in the mud with him in the middle of Hyde Park. It was past believing.

Daphne looked at her sister's stern face and sighed.

'Don't be so cross, Merva. Mr Garfield has not come near us since. He lent me his coat and I had it cleaned and pressed and sent it back to him but he did not even acknowledge its return.'

'He is probably just as shocked by his behaviour

109

as you must be,' said Minerva, starting to walk again. 'I suppose he was foxed.'

'He . . . he did apologize and he said he had had too much to drink at luncheon and . . .'

'Ah, that is it,' said the worldly-wise Minerva with satisfaction. 'I am afraid we must forgive the gentlemen when they are a trifle *well to go*. We will say no more on the subject.'

Daphne experienced a pang of disappointment, for once she had begun to talk about Mr Garfield, she really did not want to stop.

After they walked a little way in silence, Minerva said casually, 'I might send a letter to Annabelle and beg her to stay with me and bring little Charles.'

'I wish you would, Merva,' said Daphne, feeling the old comfort at having her problems solved for her by this sister who had been substitute mother for so long to the younger girls since Mrs Armitage had done nothing but drift out of one Spasm into another.

'Oh, and Betty,' said Daphne. 'You must speak to Betty, Minerva. She is not the same girl since her illness and when she is not glowering and snapping, she cries a lot. She did not wed John but she never says why. John himself hardly looks in her direction and *he* has changed. He is dressed in livery which must have cost Papa a great deal of money and he puts on *airs*.'

'Very well, I will do my best. You certainly attract a lot of attention, Daphne. Those two gentlemen over there look turned to stone. No. Don't look! You must pretend they are not there or they may think you are inviting attention. Dear, dear. They are coming towards us.'

110

'It's Mr Garfield, Merva,' said Daphne, blushing scarlet, 'and a friend.'

Minerva stopped and placed herself with the perambulator in front of Daphne and glared at the two approaching men.

She recognized Mr Garfield as he drew nearer, looking very cool and elegant. By contrast his friend was small and stocky with a cheerful, schoolboyish face.

Mr Garfield swept off his silk hat and bowed low. 'Miss Daphne,' he said calmly, addressing one black ringlet which was peeping round Minerva's shoulder, all he could see of Daphne. 'How charming to see you again . . . what I *can* see of you, that is.'

'*We* have not been introduced, sir,' said Minerva awfully. Mr Apsley cast a nervous glance up at Mr Garfield and tentatively pulled at his sleeve.

'Then let me effect the introductions, my love,' said a lazy voice behind Minerva.

Minerva swung around. Standing behind Daphne was the tall, elegant figure of her husband, his green eyes gleaming with mischief.

'My love,' said Lord Sylvester, 'may I present Mr Garfield and Mr Apsley. Mr Garfield and Mr Apsley, my wife. Do you both know Miss Daphne Armitage?'

'I have not had the pleasure,' mumbled Mr Apsley.

'Then it is a pleasure you shall experience right away. Daphne, allow me to present Mr Edwin Apsley. Mr Apsley, Miss Daphne Armitage.'

'Delighted,' said Mr Apsley.

'Now that the introductions are over,' said Minerva in steely tones, 'we must allow you two gentlemen to be on your way. You will find the cock pit in *that* direction which is no doubt where your tastes lie. Sylvester, please take us home.'

'I am sure our friends would like some refreshment,' said Lord Sylvester ignoring his wife's angry stare. 'Mr Apsley, be so good as to oblige me by playing father and pushing this wretched carriage so I may have that familiar joy of taking my wife's arm in my own. Mr Garfield, will you escort Miss Daphne? We only live a short step from here ...'

Tucking his wife's hand firmly in his aim, Lord Sylvester led Minerva away. Mr Apsley seized hold of the carriage and trundled it off after them.

Mr Garfield held out his arm, which Daphne ignored. She was blushing so much, she felt as if she had been dipped in scalding water. She could imagine Mr Garfield and Mr Apsley laughing over the abandoned way she had lain down in the mud of Hyde Park and allowed herself to be kissed.

'Strange as it may seem,' came Mr Simon Garfield's cool voice, 'gentlemen are not in the way of gossiping about the sort of things that intrigue the ladies. So you see, there is no need to stand there like a beautiful beetroot, Miss Daphne.'

Torn between relief and anger, Daphne said in a stifled voice, 'We had not heard from you. We thought you had been angered in some way.'

'Not I. Shall we follow the others?'

Daphne walked along beside him, her heart beating hard.

'Bellsire and Thunderer are waiting in Hopeworth for the return of your father,' went on Mr Garfield easily. I sent a man down to start the repairs to the church. He took them with him. They went cheerfully, seeming to know they were going home. I had to send them away for my chef had threatened to quit my establishment.'

'Thank you for being so kind to them,' said Daphne, all at once forgetting her embarrassment in a burst of gratitude. 'They are really very fond of you. I wonder you could bear to part with them.'

'It was a wrench,' he said solemnly, 'but they left many mementoes behind: one chewed oriental rug, one chewed slipper, a great deal of chewed food which was meant for my guests, and the chef's chewed nerves.'

'Oh, dear. They are very high-spirited. It is because they are so *young*,' said Daphne earnestly. She looked up into his face as she spoke.

He slowed his step and looked down at her. Her cheeks were pink and her hair, peeping out from under a ridiculously frivolous bonnet, was black and shining in the sun.

The stiff breeze from the ocean moulded one side of her gown against her trim figure and he experienced such a sharp pang of naked lust that he was quite startled with himself.

He forced himself to talk easily about the goings-on in Brighton, of the various balls and parties, and how the Prince Regent was still obsessed with designing military uniforms. The poet Tom Moore, said Mr Garfield, had prophesied that the next victims of the Regent's passion for designing clothes would be his political advisers:

"Let's see," said the Regent, like Titus, perplex'd With the duties of empire, "whom shall I dress next?" So what's to be done? There's the Ministers, bless 'em! As he *made*

113

the puppets, why should he not *dress* them?'

Daphne laughed, a light rippling laugh, and Mr Apsley twisted his head nervously and looked back at them.

Mr Garfield had managed to secure Daphne's arm in his.

He chatted on about how Brighton had become a sort of West End by the sea with its half-hourly coaches, its immense promenade, its fashionable domes, bow windows and cupolas, its libraries, assembly rooms, theatres, bathing boxes; filled with the genteel and would-be genteel all enjoying what the advertisements described as 'acquatic gratification'.

How are the mighty fallen, thought Mr Apsley gloomily. Imagine Simon wasting the time of day with that simpering little miss. He'd be in parson's mousetrap soon, just like all the rest. Bachelors should stand together. Mr Apsley had taken a very strong dislike to Daphne. This dislike was shortly to be intensified.

He had been staring so hard over his shoulder, he had not been looking where he was going, and he rammed the wheels of the perambulator into the legs of a stout matron who had been placidly admiring the view. She screamed, baby Julian screamed, Minerva came running back, everyone stopped and stared.

And among everyone who stopped and stared was a young lady seated in an open landau and that young lady was none other than his faithless former mistress, Kitty. Kitty who sat and giggled at the sight of Mr Apsley, pride of the Four in Hand Club, pushing a perambulator.

Mr Apsley's shame and rage knew no bounds. It was all the fault of that Daphne-creature.

Only Lord Sylvester seemed to have any sympathy for his mortification. He took the perambulator from Mr Apsley and said, 'Is it not amazing that we famous whips cannot steer a baby's perambulator? I saw your team the other day. That's Mercer's greys you have.'

Flattered at being classed with the notable Lord Sylvester as a famous whip, Mr Apsley forgot his woes for the moment and eagerly began to describe all the people he had outbid in order to secure the greys.

By the time he had consumed a pint of iced champagne in the cool depths of Lord Sylvester's drawing room, Mr Apsley was feeling in charity with the world.

He could still not bring himself to look upon Daphne with a kind eye but he thought Minerva was a delightful and charming lady. He was further relaxed by the sight of Mr Garfield who seemed to be paying no particular attention to Daphne. Simon was a trump. *He* had never gone the way of all flesh by racing off to the altar, and why should he? There were all too many women ready to give him their favours without forcing him to marry them.

Lord Sylvester had been talking amiably about the follies of the Dandies and Dandizettes who outraged London with their elaborate and outrageous modes of dress. 'I always think it is better to set the fashion than to try to be a slave to it,' said Lord Sylvester.

'Quite right,' said Mr Apsley cheerfully. 'Now take Simon here. He don't give a fig what anyone says and I envy him for it. Even went so far as to walk a couple of curst hounds about town and would you believe it? The next day there were several of the young bloods trotting up and down with foxhounds.'

A thought struck him. 'Armitage!' he cried. 'By Jove, I sent you to a Mr Armitage at Hopeworth to buy me that couple. It wasn't the Reverend Armitage?'

'The same,' said Mr Garfield.

'Oh,' said Mr Apsley, a shadow falling across his face. 'I wondered why you was so keen to make pets out of those wretched hounds.'

'They are not wretched unless made so by callous, unfeeling treatment,' said Daphne hotly.

'Quite,' said Mr Garfield. 'Do you plan to attend the assembly tonight, Lady Sylvester?'

'No,' said Minerva. 'I did not know when Daphne would be arriving, otherwise we might have arranged to take her.'

'I will be very happy to escort her, Lady Sylvester, except that she will need a chaperone as well,' said Mr Garfield while Mr Apsley looked at him in dismay. Had Simon forgotten that they were going to play cards with the fellows at the Ship?

'In that case, my love,' said Lord Sylvester, 'I will oblige you by staying at home with Julian while you go to the ball with Daphne for a little.'

Although baby Julian had a competent nurse, not to mention a whole household of devoted servants, looking out for his welfare, Minerva and Lord Sylvester could not feel at ease unless one of them stayed home to make sure everything was all right.

Minerva bit her lip. She had told her husband of the kissing-in-the-mud on the way home and

116

Sylvester had only laughed and said the temptation was probably too great. He seemed to approve of Mr Garfield. Minerva sighed. She would much rather have stayed at home.

'Would you care to go?' she asked Daphne, hoping that young lady would refuse. Daphne looked at Mr Garfield and Mr Garfield looked at Daphne, and Daphne eventually lowered her eyes and said meekly she would like to go of all things.

'That Garfield has *hypnotized* her,' thought Minerva angrily, resolving to have a word with her husband as soon as possible.

'Oh, I say,' mumbled Mr Apsley miserably. 'Thought we was going to have an evening at the card table.'

'I had not forgotten,' said Mr Garfield equably. 'I shall no doubt join you at the Ship after I have I managed to persuade Miss Daphne to dance with me.'

Mr Apsley brightened. Simon could not very well dance more than two times with the girl or society would be outraged.

Watching his friend's expressive face, Mr Garfield reflected that Edwin was at his most tedious when he was between affairs.

Daphne watched them both and wondered what on earth the elegant and sophisticated Mr Garfield saw in the chubby, uncouth Mr Apsley. Mr Apsley looked at Daphne and wondered again what Mr Garfield could see in such a milk-and-water miss. But Mr Apsley's pulses only quickened for members of the Fashionable Impure.

CHAPTER FIVE

It was no great matter to Brighton society that Mr Garfield danced twice with Daphne Armitage at the Assembly. Her beauty created such a furore that they hardly noticed her partners. Minerva was content to sit with the dowagers and watch her sister's success. Also, since she was three months pregnant, she found she tired easily.

She had been prepared to stay very late at the ball to please Daphne, but no sooner had Daphne had her second dance with Mr Garfield than she announced herself ready to return home. Minerva's relief at being able to leave was somewhat marred to find the tall figure of Mr Garfield waiting outside to escort them. But despite her misgivings, Minerva respected her husband's judgement and put herself out to be charming to Mr Garfield, going so far as to invite him to join them at the tea tray.

Mr Garfield studied Minerva's tired face for a few moments and then said quietly that he would take his leave. Daphne, torn between relief and disappointment, watched him go.

She gave a little sigh. 'What an odd man he is, Merva. We shall not probably see him again during the rest of our stay.'

The vicar was waiting up for them and was delighted. when Minerva told him of Daphne's success. Surely Daphne would realize there were more important fish in the sea than Mr Archer.

The following day was enlivened by calls made by Daphne's new admirers. It was the custom for gentlemen to call on the lady they had danced with the night before. Of course, they could send a servant instead of calling in person, and by three in the afternoon Daphne was persuaded that that was what Mr Garfield meant to do.

She had quite given up hope—although she tried to convince herself she would be more at ease if he did *not* call—and was preparing to take the air with Minerva and baby Julian when Mr Garfield and Mr Apsley were announced.

Mr Apsley was looking slightly sullen and his scowl deepened as Mr Garfield persuaded Daphne to take a walk with him. With bad grace, Mr Apsley bethought himself of a previous engagement and walked away, looking for all the world like a sulky schoolboy.

Peregrine and James then seemed ready to accompany Mr Garfield and Daphne, and were stopped from going by Lord Sylvester who said he had an errand for them.

And so Daphne was left free to stroll along the promenade with Mr Garfield, avoiding talking to him by bowing and nodding to new acquaintances from the ball the night before.

At last Daphne began to feel herself sadly lacking in manners and turned her attention to Mr Garfield who was surveying her with a look of affectionate amusement. 'The ball was very fine,' essayed Daphne.

'Very,' he agreed, 'although I found it flat after my second dance with you.'

'Indeed?' Daphne fanned herself vigorously although there was a cool breeze blowing in from the ocean. 'Do you intend to stay in Brighton for long, Mr Garfield?'

'Ah, that depends . . .'

'On what?'

'On how long I find myself amused?'

'Are you often bored?'

'Yes, Miss Daphne, very often.'

'That is a sign of weakness,' said Daphne severely. 'People who are often bored set very high standards for other people but not for themselves. Perhaps you are bored, Mr Garfield, because you yourself are boring.'

'I am desolated you find me dull.'

'Not in the slightest. I find you uncomfortable.'

'Odso? Then what can I do to make myself more comfortable?'

'I do not know,' said Daphne, unable to analyse the unsettling feelings coursing through her body. 'Perhaps if we could talk about general things.'

'Very well. Let us talk about your father. You must be proud of his reputation as a huntsman?'

'I do not know if he is as brilliant a huntsman as he believes,' said Daphne cautiously. 'My young sister, Diana, is most interested in the sport and says that there has been a great dog fox plaguing the district for years and Papa cannot seem to be able to hunt it down despite all the money he spends on hounds and horses. He is most unconventional and wears a scarlet coat, or pink as he calls it, and parsons are only supposed to wear purple on the hunting field. Then there is that silly trap he made for Dr Philpotts.'

'He is a prime eccentric, I think,' said Mr Garfield, 'but you must not be too hard on him. It is all very well telling me these things, but do not, I pray, repeat them to anyone else in society.'

'Why?'

'Well,' he said gently, 'it is not right to criticize

120

members of your family, in my opinion, although many of the *ton* do just that. Also they gossip a good deal—malicious gossip. It is a slight thing, but they would enjoy spreading the rumour that Mr. Armitage was a failure as a huntsman. His extravagance would be largely condemned and his life made a misery. He is very proud of his reputation, I think.'

'Surely no one would trouble to gossip about a country vicar.'

'Your father is no ordinary vicar. He has startled society by marrying three of his daughters off to the highest prizes on the Marriage Mart. That sort of thing creates jealousy. The world and his wife would be only too glad to find something they could sneer about. There are many match-making mamas who detest your father and feel their prize darlings could have secured at least one highly eligible man had it not been for the Armitage sisters. In fact the Armitage sisters seem to have a genius for securing the affections of dyed-in-the-wool bachelors.'

'Like yourself?' Daphne blushed miserably as soon as the words were out of her mouth.

'Miss Daphne,' he said softly, turning his back to the glittering sea and taking both her gloved hands in his own. 'I am very much a bachelor, or at least I have always considered myself the sort of man who would never marry. Perhaps it is because I never met anyone who could . . .'

'Yoo-hoo!'

Both swung round, each wondering who could be hailing either one of them in such a vulgar manner.

A pretty lady, somewhat over-painted about the mouth and over-plunging about the neckline, was waving to Mr Garfield from an open carriage. Even

121

the unworldly Daphne recognized her as belonging to the Fashionable Impure.

She turned her head resolutely away.

'Simon!' came a feminine scream. 'Help me down, John. *Simon!*' The voice came nearer. 'I could not believe my eyes.'

'Madam, I have never seen you in my life before.' Mr Garfield's voice dripped ice and Daphne gave a little sigh of relief and turned back. The lady had been helped down by her coachman. Gathering the long train of her muslin gown over one arm, she tripped up to Mr Garfield.

'In case you did not hear me, madam,' said Mr Garfield looking stonily down at her, 'I have never seen you before.'

'Oh!' The lady let out a strangled gasp and raised a scented handkerchief to her mouth. 'How could you say such a thing? When I have been in your protection for two years.'

Daphne felt herself go hot with embarrassment. The lady could not be acting. Her distress appeared genuine. And being a bachelor, thought Daphne gloomily, did not mean being celibate.

'Simon.' The pretty lady was now clutching at Mr Garfield's coat. 'Do not spurn me. You have not come nigh me for two weeks. Is *she* the reason?'

Daphne started to walk away.

Mr Garfield's voice stopped her. 'Stay, Miss Daphne,' he said. 'Now, madam,' he went on, turning to the lady and prising her hands free of his coat, 'you have five seconds to turn around and go back to your carriage before I call the watch.'

'Simon!'

'One!'

'Oh, miss'—to Daphne—'don't you have nothing

122

to do with him. Only see how he spurns me.'

'Two.'

'If you knew what he did to me . . .'

'Three, four, five,' snapped Mr Garfield, and then raising his voice, he called, 'Watch! Hey, watchman!'

The lady ran back to her carriage so fast, she seemed like a coloured blur to the transfixed Daphne. She called urgently to her coachman and the carriage set off at a smart pace.

Mr Garfield seized Daphne's arm in a rough grip and started to hustle her towards a hackney carriage.

'Leave me alone!' cried Daphne furiously. 'To be subjected . . .'

'Shut up,' said Mr Garfield coldly. 'Driver, keep that carriage in sight and see where it goes. If you do not lose it there will be a guinea for you.'

'Now, listen to me,' said Mr Garfield, taking Daphne's hands in a tight clasp. 'No, don't turn your head away. I have never seen that lady in my life before. We are going to follow her, and with luck, we will find out who put her up to this mischief.'

'I could swear she was genuine,' said Daphne. 'Please let me go. You are hurting me. You have no right to embroil me in your affairs. They are of no interest to me, sir.'

'That woman was an actress or I'll eat my hat. Do stop making a fuss, Miss Daphne.'

'But we are in a *closed* carriage, sir. You will cause a scandal.'

'Damme, so we are,' he said, staring haughtily about the cramped inside of the hack. 'Oh, well, you'll just have to marry me.'

'I seem to be unlucky in that the proposals of marriage I receive are decidedly off-hand,' snapped Daphne.

'Do be quiet,' he said, craning his neck. 'That carriage has just drawn up at the Ship. Ah, I begin to see who is behind this. Come along, Miss Daphne. You are the sort of young miss who will damn me for life unless you have ironbound proof of my innocence.'

Still protesting, Daphne nonetheless allowed herself to be escorted into the Ship.

In a corner of the coffee room was Mr Apsley. He had just risen to his feet. The lady who had accosted Mr Garfield was talking volubly to Mr Apsley, who suddenly looked over the top of her bonnet and saw Mr Garfield and Daphne framed in the doorway of the coffee room.

He turned brick red.

'So that's that,' said Mr Garfield, leading Daphne back out of the inn.'

'That's *what?*' said Daphne crossly.

'You are remarkably thick-witted, my love. Was it not obvious or must I take you back and punch my dear friend's head before your eyes? That little ladybird was put up to the scene just enacted on the promenade by Edwin.'

'You must call him out.'

'How bloodthirsty you are. The scandal would ruin both of us. No, I shall deal with Edwin in my own way.'

'And he is supposed to be your *friend.*'

'He is a silly man who has no female to engage his attentions at the moment and thinks he sees one of his oldest and most valued friends falling in love.'

'He *is* very silly, is he not?' said Daphne, rather

124

breathlessly. Mr Garfield was looking at her in such an odd way.

He was actually looking down at Daphne and wondering how he could be so easily bewitched by beauty when he had already known so much of it.

'Our walk is not spoiled,' he said. 'I refuse to let it be marred by Edwin's malice. We will pretend that nothing happened and that we have just started out. Do observe that dreadful quiz over there.'

He led her off along the sunny street, conversing lightly, talking nonsense, until Daphne began to relax. She could not feel completely at ease in his company, however, because she was overcome by a longing to feel his lips against hers once more. Her colour came and went. She was conscious of every movement of his tall body, of the caressing note in his voice. She thought fleetingly of Cyril Archer and then banished him resolutely to the back of her mind.

When they reached Minerva's house, Mr Garfield came to a monumental decision. He was tired of searching his feelings, analysing his feelings. All he knew was that he wanted Daphne Armitage as he had never wanted any other woman in the whole of his life.

Almost abruptly he said, 'Tell your father I will pay a call on him tomorrow morning.'

'Yes,' Daphne whispered, her heart beating hard.

'You can guess what I wish to ask him, Daphne,' said Mr Garfield, looking down at her intently. 'May I hope your answer will be "yes" if I find favour with him?'

Daphne looked up into his strange yellow eyes. There was a glow in them that made every nerve in her body tingle.

She did not know if she loved him. But she knew if she refused him then she might never see him again. And that was suddenly past bearing.

She slowly nodded her head.

He raised her hand to his lips and then strode off down the street.

Daphne watched him until he was out of sight and then ran into the house.

She must speak to her father immediately. 'Merva! Where's Papa?' she cried, removing her bonnet and swinging it by the strings.

'I am afraid Papa had to go to Hopeworth. He will return as soon as possible,' said Minerva, looking up from her sewing. 'It is a suicide, you see. Poor Miss Jenkins.'

'Oh dear,' said Daphne. Miss Jenkins was a spinster of the parish of Hopeworth. It was known that she had very little money, and everyone had tried to help her, but Miss Jenkins' gentility and pride were as strong as her poverty and she would not accept charity. She had been very odd of late, walking about the village and talking to herself.

The reason for the vicar's abrupt departure was this. The burial of a suicide or 'self-murderer' was a relic of a more barbarous age and yet, despite many protests, it still clung on. The suicide had to be buried at a crossroads and a stake driven through the body to fasten it to the ground—'of the earth, earthy'—and thus prevent its perturbed spirit from wandering about.

Although the curate, Mr Pettifor, was very happy to perform the vicar's duties when that clergyman was absent from the parish, the poor man baulked at the burial of a suicide and had fainted clean away at the last one.

126

Therefore the vicar had to return.

'I particularly wanted to talk to Papa,' said Daphne. 'You see, Merva . . .'

'You have not noticed,' said Minerva quietly. 'We have a visitor.'

The blinds were drawn against the sun, casting the far corner of the room into shadow. Out of the shadow stepped Mr Cyril Archer, his lips curled in his usual beautiful smile and his eyes as empty as the summer sky outside.

Daphne thought desperately of appealing to Minerva for help, then she stiffened her spine. She had led Mr Archer to believe they would be married. She must deal with the matter herself. She must tell him in the kindest way possible that now she could not.

'Minerva,' said Daphne, 'I must have a few minutes alone with Mr Archer, if you please. You may leave the door open.'

'Very well,' said Minerva, gathering up her sewing. 'I shall be in the morning room if you need me.'

Daphne, rather pale, faced Mr Archer. He was examining the polish on the toes of his boots with evident satisfaction.

'Mr Archer,' said Daphne, very loudly, as if talking to the deaf. *'Mr Archer!'*

'Yes, my love?' Mr Archer wrenched his gaze away from his boots and fixed his vacant eyes on Daphne's tense face.

'Mr Archer, it grieves me and pains me to have to tell you this, but I cannot marry you.'

For a moment something angry, sly and cunning peeped out of Mr Archer's eyes. It was like seeing an evil face looking out of the window of a beautiful

127

house. And then he was his usual empty-faced self again.

'But I am afraid you must,' he said over his shoulder, strolling to the fireplace and picking a figurine up from the mantel. He turned it over and examined the mark on its base with great interest.

'You really must listen to me,' said Daphne, becoming irritated. *I am not going to marry you.*

'But you shall,' said Mr Archer, still examining the figurine. 'Because, an you do not, then the whole of London will hear of your family's shame.'

'Fustian! There is no scandal in our family.'

'There is. A very great one. How think your sister Annabelle came by that brat?'

Daphne clenched her fists and said in a hard little voice, 'Pray leave this minute, sir.'

'Oh, no. You will listen to me or you will regret it to your dying day. I overheard your father say quite distinctly, and I quote, "I know what ails Brabington. It was because I was able to give you a child and he cannot!"'

'Nonsense,' said Daphne, breathing hard. 'Go ahead and tell your tale. You will be taken to court by my father—and may you spend the rest of your days in Bedlam.'

'But you see, I am very confident. Only think, Daphne, of that squat little baby and think of your father. Think also that Brabington cannot bear to look at the child.'

'No. It can't be true.'

'But it is. I am not the fool you take me for. Incest. And by a vicar. You would be written up in all the history books.'

Daphne sat down suddenly. Mr Archer looked so confident, so sure of himself.

'You do not think I would dare say such a thing were it not true,' he persisted. 'Your brothers-in-law are very powerful, not to mention leaders of the *ton*.'

Daphne's lips moved in a soundless prayer. It could *not* be true.

'I will ask my father,' she said boldly.

'Yes, do that,' said Mr Archer. 'I have no doubt he will deny it, but you may judge of his innocence by his reaction. I will not wait very long. Should I hear, for example, that you are encouraging the attentions of another man, then I shall not hesitate to spread my story.'

'Go now,' said Daphne, forcing herself to be calm. 'I will write to you as soon as I have spoken to my father. It will mean I have to travel to Hopeworth so you must give me time.'

'I will wait to hear from you,' said Mr Archer. 'Do you not like my cravat? It is mine own invention. I call it the Archer.'

Daphne gave a stifled exclamation and ran from the room.

Her first impulse was to flee to the morning room and bury her aching head in Minerva's lap and pour out the whole story. But Minerva would promptly tell Lord Sylvester, Lord Sylvester would go in pursuit of Mr Archer and then the whole horrible story would be out. She could never marry Mr Garfield now. But surely it would turn out to be a monstrous lie. Her own father. Her own sister. It was past belief.

But although Daphne had been out in society for a very little while, she had already heard some very scandalous *on dits*. Then there had been a case of incest in Hopeworth. The girl was sent away but people talked in whispers. It was an old story. It had happened long before Daphne was born, but people still talked about it.

Daphne did not know the full meaning of incest because she did not know how babies were conceived. Her mind flinched from thinking about it, like one flinches from nameless horrors.

Her head felt hot and sore and she would dearly have loved to climb into bed and close her eyes and lose her worries in sleep.

Instead, she sat down at the toilet table and rearranged her hair in an elaborate style and carefully rouged her face. Minerva must be persuaded that the sudden decision to return to Hopeworth was nothing more than a rather irritating girlish whim.

*   *   *

The vicar leaned wearily on his shovel. He mopped his brow and looked up at the churchyard cross, silhouetted against the starry sky.

'Are you quite finished, Charles?' came the squire's voice. 'If we stay here much longer, we will be discovered and accused of being resurrection men.'

'Well, we are body-snatchers after all,' grinned the vicar. 'But we're only taking Miss Jenkins' body to a holy place.'

'You are a brave man, Charles. It is dirty work.'

'As far as I am concerned, it is God's work,' said the vicar earnestly. 'I cannot in my heart of hearts believe He wants a poor soul like Miss Jenkins to rest at the Hopeworth crossroads with a stake through her heart. But Lor', she was a bony one!

130

It was hard enough driving that stake home, but a demmed sight harder to pull it out.'

The vicar had buried Miss Jenkins in her dishonoured grave that very afternoon to the satisfaction of the whole village, who had turned out to watch the ghastly proceedings. But the Reverend Charles Armitage could never believe anyone driven to their death by poverty and humiliation a sinner. And so he had felt he could not rest quietly in his bed until he had dug up the body of Miss Jenkins, removed the cruel stake, and had taken her body to a quiet corner of the old churchyard for a Christian burial.

'Carriage on the road,' hissed the squire. 'Get down.'

'No need to. We're finished,' said the vicar. 'If anyone asks, I'll say I couldn't sleep and came to tidy the graves.'

The squire screwed his eyes up in an effort to see better as the carriage rolled past.

'I think there was a crest on the panel,' he said. 'Perhaps one of your daughters is arriving late.'

'I should have stayed in Brighton,' grumbled the vicar. 'Daphne and Garfield were smellin' of April and May when I left. But something in my bones is telling me that's Daphne coming home.'

'I would very much like to go home myself, Charles,' said the little squire. 'Robbing graves late at night does not do my rheumatics any good.'

'Let's hope we don't have to do it again,' said the vicar gloomily. 'The next old beldame in the village who won't accept food 'cos she's too proud is going to have it forced down her throat. Goodnight Jimmy. Why not share a bite of dinner with me tomorrow?'

The squire repressed a shudder at the thought of the vicarage cooking. 'It is most kind of you, Charles, but Ram is preparing one of his special curries.' Ram was the squire's Indian servant.

'Really hot?' asked the vicar wistfully.

'Very hot. You are welcome to share it with me.'

'That's kind of you. Thankee,' said the vicar eagerly.

They parted at the lych-gate.

The vicar recognized Lord Sylvester Comfrey's carriage standing outside the vicarage.

The lamps in the parlour had been lit. When he pushed open the door of the parlour, Daphne rose to meet him. She had shadows of fatigue under her eyes. She signalled to the maid, Betty, to retire and waited until the housekeeper, Mrs Hammer, had set down the tea tray.

'Have you told Mrs Armitage you are home?' asked the vicar.

'No, nor Diana. I am very tired and would simply like to have a dish of tea and go to bed. But I am glad to see you, Papa.'

The vicar moved forward to embrace her and then stopped short as Daphne shrank back in her chair.

'Do not touch me,' she said in a quiet, even voice. 'There is something I must ask you.'

'Very well,' said the vicar. 'Go on.'

'I understand that Annabelle's baby is not Brabington's,' said Daphne, pouring tea with every appearance of composure.

The vicar sat down heavily. Daphne raised her large eyes and studied him intently. Inside she was praying desperately that he would exclaim, be shocked, tell her she was talking nonsense.

132

But he said nothing for what seemed an age. Then he said, 'So you know,' and taking out a handkerchief, he mopped his brow. 'Well,' he added with a weary sigh, 'I had better explain.'

Daphne looked at her father with a sort of terrible pity. 'No, Papa,' she said, putting down her tea cup, rising and walking to the door. The matter is closed. You may congratulate me. I am to wed Mr Archer.'

'But Daphne . . .'

Daphne went out and quietly closed the door behind her.

Summer had fled before a chill wind. The sea was steel grey. Everything was grey. Grey sky, grey buildings, grey people.

Mr Garfield walked alone along the promenade at Brighton.

He had called again on Lord Sylvester, only to be told that neither Mr Armitage nor Daphne had returned.

Pride stopped him from asking Minerva whether Daphne had told her of his proposal of marriage. For it *had* been a proposal, he thought savagely. He *had* told her he would call on her father the next day.

Sharp, angry waves thudded on the beach and a seagull screamed overhead.

The Brighton Season was over. The Fashionables had already packed up and returned to London to prepare for the rigours of the Little Season. Even Mr Apsley had left, nursing a sore jaw, a reminder not to interfere in his friend's affairs again.

Why had she left without a word? Mr Garfield turned the problem over and over in his head. Had she believed that silly actress that Edwin had hired?

It was evident she had changed her mind, and yet he had been so sure she was not indifferent to him.

Then he saw, too late, that the Colonel and Mrs Cartwright were bearing down on him. They had been late arrivals to the seaside resort, the colonel having been persuaded by his doctor that the sea breezes would alleviate the pain of a disordered spleen.

'Afternoon, Garfield,' said the colonel. 'Surprised to find you still here. We'll all be damned as Unfashionables if we stay much longer.'

'The Prince Regent is still with us,' pointed out Mr Garfield.

'Ah, yes, indeed,' said the colonel, turning and saluting the Royal Pavilion.

'I was most startled at the news in the papers this morning,' said Mrs Cartwright. 'Do you remember Miss Daphne Armitage? The young lady who cooked dinner at Lady Godolphin's?'

'Yes,' said Mr Garfield, with seeming indifference.

'She is to wed Mr Cyril Archer, you know, that rather stupid young man. Very handsome, of course, but her sisters made their name by marrying looks *and* brains *and* fortune.'

'I have heard that rumour before.' Mr Garfield looked out to sea with a little shrug of his broad shoulders as if dismissing the matter from his mind. 'But it is not a rumour. It is in all the London journals as well as the Brighton ones. Do you think she has made a wise choice? I did not quite *take* to that young man, if you know what I mean.'

'Yes, I know what you mean.' Mr Garfield sounded unutterably weary. He raised his hand briefly to the brim of his beaver hat and strolled off

134

down the promenade.

So she is like all the others, he thought, feeling anger begin to mount inside his head. Marry Archer! Daphne Armitage was empty, silly and vain. He thought he had sensed a rich seam of honesty and courage and decency in her. What a fool he had been. He had been bewitched by a large pair of eyes, a trim figure, and hair as black as midnight.

He reminded himself he had business to attend to in London, business which would occupy all his mental energies. Mr Garfield came from an old aristocratic family and yet he had plunged into the world of trade some ten years ago, shortly after his twenty-first birthday, and had built up a prosperous concern, importing goods from the Far East.

The world of the City fascinated him more than the world of the West End.

He had neglected his duties sadly of late . . . and all over a silly little girl.

CHAPTER SIX

By the time the Little Season had begun, the brief, blazing glory that had been the animated Daphne Armitage of Brighton had flashed like a comet across the social scene and burned out.

People who had attended a very long and very boring opera just to get a glimpse of the latest Armitage pearl pronounced themselves vastly disappointed.

She was like a wax doll. Mr Archer, as everyone already knew, was like something out of Madame

135

Tussaud's. So much beauty, they mourned. Alas, that it lacked the spirit to set it alight.

Daphne was once more armoured against the cruel world in careful fashion and a mask-like face. She rarely smiled, or cried, or showed any animation whatsoever. Heartless society said it could only be grateful that two such beautiful pieces of empty vanity had found each other, thereby sparing some unfortunate from marrying either one of them. Mr Archer was always straightening his waistcoat, or fiddling with his cravat, and Miss Daphne was always studying her face in a hand mirror to make sure some small spot or errant strand of hair was not marring the flawless perfection of her face.

Before, she had at least appeared charming in her silence. There had been something fresh and appealing about her. Now she looked as if a vital force had shrivelled and died within.

Mr Garfield, emerging briefly from his City labours for one last look at his lost love, heaved a sigh of relief and congratulated himself on a narrow escape. But he longed for the pretty, vital girl he thought he had loved, said a few mourning words over her bright image, and returned to his chores, feeling as if he had just attended a funeral.

The disappointed vicar had washed his hands of the whole affair. Certainly, he had promised God that Daphne could marry whom she chose. But Mr Armitage could not help feeling He had a warped sense of humour, and once more the vicar's prayers became mechanical and the beauty of the cold, crisp mornings no longer moved him.

Minerva was disappointed in Daphne but not very much surprised. She had never known Daphne very well, having been more concerned with the older girls. Minerva was still rather moralistic and assumed anyone as vain as Daphne appeared to be must be remarkably devoid of sensibility. It was just as well Daphne had not formed a tendre for the elusive Mr Garfield as it had once seemed she had. He was too vital and masculine a man to settle for a pretty doll.

Only Lady Godolphin began to wonder if there was not something very serious troubling Daphne. Daphne was not to be wed until the following year—Mr Archer being quite comfortable with the engagement—and there was no great fuss about her debut in the Little Season since she was already engaged. No one in their right mind ever put out a great deal of money on a daughter who was already off the lists.

The vicar and Mrs Armitage, together with Diana and Frederica, remained at Hopeworth. Daphne was lodged with Lady Godolphin at her house in Hanover Square. A sum of money had been paid to that lady to chaperone Daphne to various social events, Minerva and Annabelle being too taken up with their babies to find time for the social round.

Lady Godolphin found it a very undemanding sort of job. Mr Archer would always arrive on time, beautifully dressed, to meet Daphne, who was always on time, and always beautifully dressed, and then she would proceed to accompany them to whatever rout or ball she had selected for them since they seemed to have no preference of their own.

Off they would set, hardly speaking, Daphne sent on her way by the now perpetually bitter and sullen maid, Betty.

During her first week back in London, Daphne had certainly caused one night's alarm by screaming in her sleep about insects. Lady Godolphin had had Daphne's bedroom almost buried under an avalanche of Keating's powder in an attempt to soothe the girl.

But what had sharpened Lady Godolphin's senses to Daphne's underlying distress and despair was when her ladyship fell in love again. And nothing sharpens the senses so much as unrequited love.

They were to attend a rout that evening at the Brothers' mansion in Portland Square. Lady Godolphin usually avoided routs these days, damning them as a waste of time. Perhaps some other members of London society thought the same, but it did not stop them from attending in great numbers.

And there was something very exhausting and quite mad about a society rout.

Great assemblies were called routs or parties, although the invitation only said simply that such and such a person would be *at home*.

The house in which the rout was to take place was stripped from top to bottom; beds, drawers and all but ornamental furniture being carried out of sight, to make room for a crowd of well-dressed people received at the door of the principal apartment by the mistress of the house whose job it was to smile at every newcomer as if they were a long lost friend.

Nobody sat: there was no conversation, nor cards, nor music; 'only elbowing, turning and winding from room to room'. Then at the end of quarter of an hour you had to battle down the crowded staircase you had battled up such a short time ago and then stand freezing on the threshold, spending more time with the footmen than you had done with their masters upstairs, as you waited for your carriage to be brought around.

Ten o'clock, the time Lady Godolphin and her small party set out, was the time of day when fashionable London really came to life. Everything that had gone on earlier was a sort of overture to this grand moment.

For social London did not begin to stir out of doors until four in the afternoon. Apart from the milk maids and the other street vendors, the only sound to be heard earlier was the drum and military music of the Guards, marching from their barracks in Hyde Park; at the head of the procession, four negro giants crashing cymbals.

After paying calls and lounging in Bond Street, society returned at six to change for dinner. At six the street lights were lit; a long line of bright dots which hardly did anything to dispel the gloom.

Then at eight the first wave of carriages rumbled across the cobbles, two wavering red flames of light like eyes in the front of each. The very way in which your footman alighted to knock on the door was a social art. As the American visitor, Louis Simond, described it: 'Stopping suddenly, a footman jumps down, runs to the door, and lifts the heavy knocker—gives a grcat knock—then several smaller ones in quick succession—then with all his might—flourishing as on a drum, with an art, and an air, and a delicacy of touch, which denotes the quality, the rank, and the fortune of his master.'

For two hours there was a pause, and then at ten

o'clock the noise of carriages in the cobbled streets became deafening.

The Brothers' mansion blazed with light, all the curtains back and the blinds up.

Daphne was wearing the very latest thing in acrostic hats. That is the hat was embellished with silk flowers which spelled out the letters of her name—dahlia, aster, peony, hyacinth, narcissus and eglantine. Her gown was of blue and white striped gauze and her bare shoulders kept warm with a pereline of richly embroidered muslin.

Lady Godolphin was wearing a round gown of vivid green cambric cut low enough to expose what seemed like an acre of withered flesh in front and behind. Her squat neck boasted a necklace of rather dirty diamonds, and she wore a turban with two striped feathers waving about the top and looking as if they did not belong there—which, in fact, they did not, Lady Godolphin having thrust them in at the last minute.

Mr Archer was very correct in knee breeches and swallow tail coat with his *chapeau bras* tucked under his arm. Lady Godolphin told him he looked quite tunnish, which made that gentleman glance at his own waistline in an alarmed way as if expecting to find he had sprouted an embonpoint overnight.

Lady Godolphin could only marvel at the way her two charges negotiated their way through the crowd seemingly indifferent to everyone and everything.

When they were pushing their way downstairs against the tide of people pushing up, Lady Godolphin all of a sudden came chest to chest with Colonel Arthur Brian, her late inamorato who had so callously left her for the charms of a vulgar Cit.

She tried to edge past, turning her head away and giving him the cut direct, but a very fat couple chose that moment to come abreast and so Lady Godolphin was pressed up nearly as close to the colonel as she had ever been.

'I think we should recognize each other,' said the colonel. 'It breaks my heart to see you cut me so.'

'Philanthropist!' hissed Lady Godolphin.

Colonel Brian had had quite a lot of experience when it came to translating Lady Godolphin's malapropisms. He realized his lady-love meant 'philanderer'.

'You started it all,' he said in a maddeningly reasonable tone of voice, 'when you deserted me for that young jackanapes.'

'But then you went off with that fat Cit,' grated Lady Godolphin. 'Allow me to pass.'

'No, I shall not,' said Colonel Brian, becoming agitated. 'Our separation has all been very silly.'

'Silly, heh?' Lady Godolphin drew up her massive bosom until it stuck out like a figurehead. 'Let me past, sirrah!'

'Never!'

'People is staring and you is becoming historical.'

The fat couple squeezed on ahead. With surprising speed and agility, Lady Godolphin nipped past the spare figure of the elderly colonel and lumbered down the stairs.

She was looking forward to having a deliciously impassioned scene with the colonel to enliven the tedium of waiting for her carriage—for surely he would pursue her.

Great was her dismay when she eventually looked back to find Colonel Brian had gained the top of the stairs and was *smirking* down into the cleavage of a lady who was nothing more than laced mutton.

All the old pain and anguish returned, and Lady Godolphin brooded on the doorstep of the Brothers' mansion like some massive bulldog which has just seen its bone being snatched away by an ancient poodle.

The idea of spending the rest of the fashionable night walking up and down her own bedroom dismayed her ladyship. There was a ball at the Ruthfords'. The Duke and Duchess had sent out invitations some weeks ago to which Lady Godolphin in her usual slapdash way had not replied. But if they turned up about twelve-thirty, the Duke and Duchess would no longer be receiving the guests and so would not be immediately around to make remarks about impolite and inconsiderate people.

'We're going to the Ruthfords'. Best get home and change,' growled Lady Godolphin. 'We'll set you down and you can call for us later, Mr Archer.'

'I had not meant to go out again,' said Daphne. 'Then mean it,' snapped Lady Godolphin. 'I'm fair wore to the bone squirin' you pair o' waxworks about so the least you can do is obleege *me*.'

A flicker of pain crossed Daphne's beautiful eyes and then was gone.

Her sensitivity heightened by her own distress, Lady Godolphin noticed the look, and noticed for almost the first time that Daphne Armitage was not entirely the unfeeling, empty-headed doll she had believed her to be.

Something impelled her to give Daphne's hand a squeeze, and, by the flickering lights of the parish lamps outside, Lady Godolphin surprised the shine

142

of tears in Daphne's large eyes.

'I do hope your carriage will not be long,' said Mr Archer. 'I have a speck of soot on my cravat.'

Lady Godolphin suddenly decided she had had more than enough of Mr Archer for one evening. 'I know you wanted to go on to the Alvaney rout, Mr Archer,' she said. 'Rumour has it the Prince Regent will be there. So why don't you take yourself?'

The carriage arrived and Mr Archer climbed in after the ladies, wondering when it could be that he had voiced a desire to go to Alvaney's since he could not remember having said at any time that he would like to go to any particular event. But he had treated himself to a new swansdown waistcoat and it would be fine if he could catch the eye of the Prince Regent. Mr Archer had all but forgotten in his immense vanity that he had coerced Daphne Armitage into becoming engaged to him. She was all he had dreamt she would be as a fiancée: cool, aloof, and very, very fashionable. Not only did she seem uninterested in his occasional dutiful and chaste caresses but actually seemed to shrink from them. So in the dim workings of his brain he finally decided that, yes, it would be splendid to go, and quite safe to leave Daphne with Lady Godolphin. He allowed himself to be set down at his lodgings and barely remembered to raise his hand in farewell, so absorbed had he already become in planning his toilet.

There was a silence as Lady Godolphin's carriage rolled on.

'Did you see him?' asked Lady Godolphin at length.

'Mr Garfield? No,' said Daphne.

'Now why should I be talkin' about Garfield?' exclaimed Lady Godolphin. 'I mean Arthur. Colonel Brian.'

'No,' said Daphne. She walked in a dark world of her own misery and hardly ever looked outside.

'A fine figure of a man,' sighed Lady Godolphin. 'I do not understand men. Just when you expect them to chase you and ask you what the matter is —well, that's the time they goes off on their lone as if they didn't care tuppence.'

'I think if anyone was really in love then they *would* ask what the matter was,' said Daphne, showing more animation than she had done since her engagement.

'Not if they thought they had been *sponged*,' said Lady Godolphin gloomily. 'The gentlemen do so hate to be sponged. Hell hath no fury like . . .'

'Scorned?'

'I said that. A pox on all men. Great lot o' follicles. Here we are arrived. Put on that pretty silver ballgown, Daphne, and for heaven's sake, do loosen yourself a bit.'

'I do not wear stays, my lady.'

'Only on your soul,' said Lady Godolphin tartly. 'Or are you really as empty as you appear?'

All Daphne's defences rose at the insult and she turned a perfectly blank face on Lady Godolphin. 'I do not know what you mean,' she said.

But Lady Godolphin *did* notice when they set out later that Daphne's hair *was* dressed in a looser, prettier and less fashionable style with only a single red silk rose against the black of her hair as an ornament. She was not wearing her silver ballgown, but a simple sprigged muslin embellished with cherry ribbons.

144

This was not due to any 'loosening' on Daphne's part, but rather to the absence of the maid, Betty. A chambermaid had helped prepare Daphne for the rout, but she was reluctant to summon further help from the servants in preparing her for the ball in case Lady Godolphin should come to hear of Betty's neglect of her duties. Betty had been missing for at least two days and Daphne had put it down to a fit of the sulks, imagining Betty remaining belowstairs. To complain to Mice and demand Betty's presence would also mean Lady Godolphin would learn of it. Daphne felt a close loyalty to the maid from the vicarage and knew that Lady Godolphin could have a very sharp tongue when it came to dealing with lax servants.

Daphne could see no escape from her own misery. It seemed to her that nothing could be done and that she must bear the burden of the terrible secret alone. If she confided in her elder sisters, then they would promptly tell their husbands, and the secret might come leaping out all over town. She could not even sit down and face the matter calmly and reasonably, for it would mean facing up to all sorts of horrors from which her virginal mind shrank. She felt perpetually tired, but always forced herself to look her best, feeling sure that if she looked beautiful, then people would leave her alone. She was so worried and so deeply depressed, she could not even summon up any hate for Mr Archer.

When they reached the ball she meant to dance every dance so that she would be exhausted enough by the time they returned home to fall into a dreamless sleep.

There was still enough of the bewildered child

in Daphne to make her feel responsible for her father's evil. If only she had been a better daughter then perhaps Papa might not . . . But the mind could not even begin to picture what Papa had done.

She retreated very much into herself as she faced the glare of light from hundreds of wax candles and mounted the stairs with Lady Godolphin.

Lady Godolphin was once more resplendent in full war-paint. Her bosom and face was covered with a thick white coat of *blanc* and two flaming circles of rouge stood out bravely on her cheeks. She had put kohl around her eyes and covered herself in a whole deluge of *Miss In Her Teens*.

Daphne demurely entered the ballroom, large eyes carefully devoid of expression glancing around.

Then she clutched Lady Godolphin's fat arm so hard that her ladyship startled the listening company by shrieking, 'God's Hounds!'

Her pale eyes darted about the ballroom, trying to find out what had caused the normally placid Daphne such alarm.

Annabelle was there, a radiant and beautiful Annabelle, flirting quite outrageously, and seemingly totally unaware of the fact that her husband, the Marquess of Brabington, had just entered by the opposite door. Then there was that Mr Garfield. He was staring at Daphne with a rather fixed look.

And over by one of the long windows, engaged in conversation with the Duchess of Ruthfords, was Colonel Arthur Brian. Lady Godolphin decided Daphne's alarm had been caused by a spasm of fellow feeling at the sight of the colonel.

'Pretend you haven't seen him,' hissed Lady

146

Godolphin, and Daphne, thinking she meant Mr Garfield, followed her advice and looked the other way.

Never had Daphne or Lady Godolphin been more energetic than they were at that ball. Lady Godolphin had always been a prime favourite and Daphne sparkled and laughed and flirted as she had never done before. Her calm mask had slipped and she looked alive and radiant, although it was really just another kind of mask to show Mr Garfield that she did not care, and to avoid even thinking about Annabelle.

The evening wore on through supper, through quadrilles and waltzes, Scotch reels and gallops.

Not once did Colonel Brian ask Lady Godolphin to dance and not once did Mr Garfield approach Daphne.

Suddenly it was five in the morning and Daphne and Lady Godolphin, meeting at a corner of the ballroom after a very energetic country dance, realized that neither Mr Garfield nor the colonel was anywhere to be seen.

'I am totally eshausticuted,' said Lady Godolphin, fanning herself wearily. 'Do you wish to go home, Daphne?'

'Please,' said Daphne. She felt exhausted and miserable and very disappointed.

They trailed wearily out to the carriage.

'Well, my heart is broke,' sighed Lady Godolphin. 'I hope you never know what it is, Daphne, to pine and pine for a fellow and have that fellow look at you as if you was the wall.'

A stifled sob escaped Daphne and Lady Godolphin gave her hand a squeeze. 'Something's eatin' away at you, Daphne, and I never noticed it before. You can tell me.'

'I *can't*,' wailed Daphne.

'Try.'

Daphne decided to voice at least one of the evils plaguing her.

'I cannot *bear* the sight of Mr Archer,' she wailed.

'Ah,' said Lady Godolphin with deep satisfaction. '*That* I can understand. You've no need to worry. I shall give him his quittance.'

'*No!*' shrieked Daphne. 'He will talk and . . .' She bit her lip.

'Wait until we get home,' said Lady Godolphin, beginning to look very worried indeed. 'Not another word. I mean to get to the bottom o' this.'

Daphne sat trembling. She *could not* tell Lady Godolphin, but, yet, the temptation was very great. One could not imagine *anything* shocking such a reprehensible old sinner.

On their arrival at Hanover Square, Lady Godolphin marched Daphne into the Green Saloon, poured out two viciously large bumpers of brandy, insisted that Daphne drink hers 'all down' and then demanded to be told everything.

Overcome by strong drink and the desire to unburden herself of her terrible secret, Daphne started to talk and Lady Godolphin listened amazed.

'*Not* your father,' said Lady Godolphin at last. 'He don't need to tool his own daughter—saving your vaginal ears, Daphne—for he don't have to. Always got someone when the fancy took him. He ain't a saint and no one's sayin' he's been faithful to your mother, but can you blame the man? You can't cuddle up to a Spasm.'

148

'*But incest!*' wailed Daphne. 'What if it's true? The only thing that gives me any hope that the baby might not be Annabelle's is the fact that she was amazing secret about her pregnancy.'

'I've never had a proper look at that baby,' said Lady Godolphin, getting to her feet. 'We'll go and have a close look at it now.'

'We can't go calling this time of night,' protested Daphne.

'It's nigh six in the morning,' said Lady Godolphin. 'The chambermaids will be about. We'll tell 'em we have a surprise of a present for baby Charles and wants to leave it at the foot of his bed. Now what will we take? I know. Just the thing.'

She rang the bell and waited impatiently until the long-suffering Mice appeared, half in and half out of his livery.

'Wrap that up,' said Lady Godolphin, waving a hand towards a picture on the wall of a ferocious-looking lion devouring its bloody prey—just the sort of thing to give any child the horrors for life.

'And have the carriage brought round,' added Lady Godolphin.

Mice sent a speaking glance at the brandy bottle but did as he was bid.

'I do hope we are not caught,' whispered Daphne as a startled chambermaid led them into the hall of the tall house in Conduit Street and led the way up the stairs.

Lady Godolphin and Daphne followed, carrying the picture between them, having dissuaded the maid from rousing any of the other servants to help them.

'Why is nurseries always at the top o' the house?' moaned Lady Godolphin.

At last they reached the nursery door. Lady Godolphin dismissed the maid with a jerk of her head. They quietly pushed open the door and crept inside.

The fire still shone with a faint red glow and the rushlight in its pierced canister beside the cradle sent little dots of light dancing over the ceiling.

They put the picture down, Lady Godolphin leaving a note she had scribbled pinned to the wrapping.

'Now, find me a candle,' she whispered. 'I'm going to take a good look at this babe.'

Daphne lit a candle in a flat stick and handed it to Lady Godolphin, who held it up high and bent over the cradle. Daphne stared down as well and her heart sank. The round, red, angry face of the baby, even in sleep, the thick black hair, the chubby fists, all reminded her of her father.

Lady Godolphin nodded her head a couple of times and blew out the candle.

Crooking her finger, she signalled Daphne to follow her from the room. They made their way softly down the stairs. They had just gained the second landing when a door opened along the corridor to the left.

'Lawks!' muttered Lady Godolphin. She looked wildly around, opened the door of a large closet, and pulled Daphne in behind her.

'So you have finally decided to return home, my lady wife,' came the Marquess of Brabington's voice.

'Oh, Peter,' they heard Annabelle yawn. 'I am so very tired, and how was I to know you were returned to town? And how was I to know you would storm out of the ball in a fit of the sulks?'

'Because you might think of me for a change,' said the marquess, 'instead of your silly, self-centred, egotistical self. I can just about bear being neglected for that ugly brat of a baby, but to have to stand at a ball and watch my wife flirting with a lot of Bond Street fribbles is something I will not countenance.'

'Tol rol,' laughed Annabelle. 'I shall do as I please.'

'Not you. Not this night, my lady. Before I leave you, you will have something to think about.'

'Peter! You ripped my gown!'

There came stifled scuffling noises and then a long silence followed by the protesting creak of a bed which sounded as if a body had just been thrown down on it from the far side of the room.

'Let us go,' muttered Lady Godolphin.

They inched their way cautiously down the stairs. When they reached the hall, a high keening wail sounded from above.

'He is murdering her,' gasped Daphne, turning to run back up the stairs again to her sister's defence.

'Not he,' grinned Lady Godolphin. 'Everything will be all right now.'

They made their way out to the carriage.

'But the baby,' wailed Daphne. 'I never noticed before how much it looks like Father!'

'Tish,' said Lady Godolphin comfortably. 'Don't look a bit like Charles. I remember your father as a young man, see. You wouldn't believe it, Daphne, but he was wonderfully slim with a dreamy sort of face and curly hair. A little pocket Adonis, he was. Peregrine and James favour him. *They* didn't look nothing like that baby when they was in their cradles, now did they?'

151

'No-o-o,' said Daphne slowly, 'but I am persuaded the baby can't be theirs. Annabelle put on such airs all the nine months but she never seemed to put on any weight. Lord Brabington is a fine man and would never ignore a son of his own in the way he ignores Charles.'

'I agree with you. But Annabelle desperately wanted a baby and somehow your father managed to supply her with one. We'll need to go cautiously until we find a way to silence Mr Archer. Now I never thought of him as a lady's man. How does he kiss you?'

'He doesn't,' said Daphne, startled. 'Well . . . he does. Here.' She pointed to her brow.

'Aha! Seems to me he wanted a bit o' decoration to get wed so he could seem like a real man. Didn't say anything 'cos you looked as if you were happy to be marrying a wax dummy, and, if you will forgive the observatory, you looked like one yourself.'

'I am so worried. What am I to do?'

'Uglify yourself for a start,' said Lady. Godolphin, 'and we'll begin by taking Mr Archer to all the unfashionable places we can think of. That way he'll start to get a disgust of you. I'll write to Charles and summon him to London. The minute we find out where that baby comes from, we can give Archer his marching orders. But if we do anything now, he'll spread that filthy story, and although that baby ain't your father's—how could you believe such a thing?—you young gels have minds like cesspools—it *would* make a stink. Anyways, we'd best find out from him where the baby comes from.'

'But I am so afraid of him . . .'

'Afraid of that man-milliner? Pooh!' Lady

Godolphin put an arm about Daphne's shoulders. 'I will take care of everything. Poor child. You have nothing to worry about now.'

Daphne quite suddenly put her head on Lady Godolphin's shoulder, gave a little smile, and fell fast asleep.

'Dear me,' said Lady Godolphin. 'You never know what goes on under a body's face. I don't know what to do until I talk to Charles. Incest, indeed! One would think the Reverend Charles Armitage was that Edith's Puss!'

Lady Godolphin's eyes began to droop and soon she was asleep as well.

* * *

The vicar of St Charles and St Jude was feeling at peace with the world as he stood on the step of Squire Radford's cottage *ornée* and said goodnight to his old friend.

Mr Armitage had enjoyed an excellent dinner and an excellent conscience. The squire had praised him warmly for putting aside mercenary considerations and allowing Daphne's engagement to go ahead. Mr Garfield's expert was doing a splendid job of restoring the church and the vicar quite forgot that he had once planned to pocket the thousand guineas himself.

The air was cold and crisp with no sign of ground frost. It promised to be an excellent hunting day on the morrow and several of the local farmers were joining the vicar and his pack in one more attempt to hunt the old dog fox down.

'Goodnight and thankee, Jimmy,' said the vicar, cramming on his shovel hat. 'I cannot recall when

153

I enjoyed a meal more.' He buttoned his coat as he spoke. One middle button found the strain across the vicar's stomach too much and popped off onto the ground.

With a muttered exclamation the vicar bent to pick it up, and, at that precise moment, a ball whistled over the top of his head, missed the startled squire by inches, and buried itself in the half-open door.

The vicar straightened up and wheeled about. He saw a rustling in the bushes by the gate.

Despite the squire's cry of warning, the vicar moved with quite amazing speed for such a small, fat man. He plunged into the bushes while the squire called to his servants for help. There was a scream and a scuffle and the vicar emerged from the bushes, dragging a female figure behind him.

'In there,' he said, thrusting a woman roughly before him into the hall of the cottage.

The squire gazed in amazement at the sullen tear-streaked face of the maid, Betty.

'You'll hang for this Betty Simpson,' growled the vicar. 'A murdering criminal, that's what you are. And ungrateful too! Trying to shoot the hand what feeds you.'

'I don't care,' sobbed Betty. 'I ain't got nothing to live for. Not since you took my baby away.'

'Charles!'

The squire started in such shock that his powdered wig fell over one eye.

All the vicar's blustering anger fled and he looked as sulky and sullen as the maid.

The squire stared wildly about at his avidly listening servants and took a firm grip on himself.

'Ram,' he ordered his Indian servant, 'take

everyone away and impress on them that they heard and saw *nothing* this evening or they will lose their employ. Charles, bring Betty into the library.'

'No need,' said the vicar hurriedly ...

'Charles,' said the squire sternly, walking to the library door and holding it open.

The vicar shuffled miserably in with Betty after him.

'Sit down both of you,' ordered the squire. He turned to Betty. 'Now, my dear,' he said gently, 'no one is going to hurt you if you tell the truth. What is this about your baby?'

'Don't,' pleaded the vicar.

'I'll tell you,' said Betty wearily. 'John Summer and me made a baby so's the master would let us marry. But that Miss Annabelle, her what's Lady Brabington now, was always going on about wanting the baby she couldn't have. My John had got into sore debt over in Hopeminster with gambling at the cockpit. Master says to John, he says, that if we give the baby to Miss Annabelle, then the debts will be paid, and a sum of money given to John besides. They both badgered me wicked, the master and John. Said my child would grow up to be a lord or a lady. Said I was selfish and unfeeling. They never let me be until I agreed. I was sent away until I had the baby and it was took from me and given to Miss Annabelle—I mean, Lady Brabington. I had to watch her trying to be a mother and not knowing how, and my boy crying and crying. Lord Brabington hated my boy. I could see that. I got so's I didn't want to live, but I thought before I went, I'd give the master the fright of his life for all the sorrow he's caused me. I never fired a gun afore and I was sure the ball wouldn't go near him.

'I'm a wicked girl, Mr Radford, but I'm that miserable, I want to die.'

Squire Radford sat down and stared at the vicar in horror.

The vicar miserably shuffled his feet. 'Didn't seem wrong at the time,' he mumbled. 'There was Bella breakin' her heart for a baby, and there was Betty like to have as many as she wanted. How was I to know she would turn agin John? I did it for the best. Women,' said the vicar passionately, 'are allus weepin' about something. Never could take them seriously.'

The squire folded his lips in a thin line. Then he said, 'Where is John Summer?'

'Up at the vicarage.'

The squire rang the bell.

'What are you going to do?' asked the vicar.

'Put this matter right,' said the squire sternly. 'Ram, go to the vicarage and bring John Summer back with you.'

When the servant had left, he turned to the vicar and Betty. 'Charles, the minute John Summer gets here, you will marry John and Betty. No. Not a word. Then you will go to London and tell Annabelle she must give the baby to Betty.'

'But the hunt!' wailed the vicar. 'Tomorrow's the hunt.'

'You nearly drive a young girl to suicide,' said the squire. 'You fail to do the decent thing by marrying them because in the first place you do not want to pay John enough to keep a wife, and in the second, you wish the baby for your daughter. Yet you pay John's debts therefore encouraging his vice of gambling. Because of Betty's agony, you nearly lose your own life. I am trying to right a terrible

156

wrong and all you can think about is hunting.'

The vicar suddenly burst into tears, knuckling his eyes with his chubby fists. 'You are right, Jimmy,' he wailed. 'I'm evil. I'm always doin' evil things. Woe is me! "For the good that I would do I do not; but the evil which I would not, that I do." Romans, chapter VII, verse 19. Soon as it's right and tight, I'll go to Philpotts and tell him to find another vicar.'

The vicar's sobs grew louder. Betty stood up, took a few steps forward, and sank to her knees in front of the vicar and put a timid hand on his sleeve.

'Don't take on so, master,' she whispered: 'I was mad. I did agree, like you said. Men don't understand these things. Don't cry, Mr Armitage. We've all been a little mad. Please don't cry. As long as I get my baby back, I'll never want for anything again.'

But the vicar's conscience was tearing him apart and he would not be comforted. The squire reflected that no one would have thought the reverend to have so much salt water in him.

Two days later, still heavy-hearted and exhausted with weeping, the vicar arrived in London and went straight to his daughter, Annabelle's.

His heart smote him when he walked into the drawing room. For once the baby was not crying, and Annabelle, very flushed and very pretty, was singing to it.

The vicar had brought Betty with him but insisted she wait outside in the carriage. He did not want her further distressed. He felt his already over-burdened conscience could not bear one straw.

157

'Papa!' cried Annabelle, running up to kiss him on the cheek. 'Do you stay with us? I know, you have come all this way just to admire your grandson.'

The vicar had thought he had cried himself out, but at those fell words, he began to cry again, great tearing sobs racking his chubby body.

Alarmed, Annabelle sent for her husband. The Marquess of Brabington strolled into the room and looked amazed at the crumpled sobbing heap that was his father-in-law.

'What on earth is the matter? My love, fetch some brandy. Come, Mr Armitage, you sound as if all your hounds have the distemper.'

'A pox on my hounds and my hunt,' cried the vicar.

The marquess began to look seriously worried. For once, baby Charles was in a high good mood and roared with laughter every time another paroxysm of sobs shook the vicar.

A servant came in with a bottle of white brandy and glasses. The vicar weakly took a gulp, blinked and drained the rest of the glass, hiccupped and stared miserably down at the floor.

'Now, Reverend,' said the marquess very gently, 'you really must let us help you in your distress.'

Annabelle turned quite white. 'A death!' she cried. 'Who is it? Minerva? Daphne?'

The vicar miserably shook his head. He gave a great gulping sob, poured another glass of brandy, drank it down and stood up and squared his shoulders.

'I am come,' he said, 'to take baby Charles back to his mother.'

'His *mother!*' exclaimed Annabelle. 'You have

discovered who she is?'

The vicar closed his eyes. He dearly wanted to lie but his terrible conscience would not let him.

'It's Betty's baby,' he said quietly. 'Our maid, Betty.'

'But why did you let us think you had brought the baby from a foundling hospital?' wailed Annabelle. 'I have tried and tried to love the poor mite as if it were my own, but Charles cries and cries. He probably *knows* his mother is missing him.'

'You appear to have caused everyone a great deal of distress,' said the marquess, 'but I confess I am relieved to know that Charles will be returning to his mother. Annabelle has been behaving so badly. I did not know what had made her change so much. But she told me the other night that she was determined to be as good a mother as Minerva, and the more the baby cried, the more she thought she was a failure. In fact, *both* Annabelle and I have been hurting each other quite dreadfully.'

He put his arm about his wife and pulled her close to him. 'We discovered the other night, my Annabelle,' he said softly, 'that we are more in love with each other than ever we were. Will you break your heart if Betty has her boy back?'

Annabelle blushed and shook her head. 'I have felt so guilty. I thought the child would never love me, and it was because I was useless as a mother and therefore as a woman. How could you persuade Betty to do such a thing, Papa? Surely the boy is John Summer's. I would have thought you would have *made* them marry each other.'

'They are married now,' said the vicar heavily. 'Betty's outside. I'll fetch her in.'

The marquess and Annabelle looked at each

159

other. 'I hope you are not distressed by this, my sweeting,' he said.

'It is a little hard to part with him,' sighed Annabelle. 'But he did cry so much and he was always so *angry*. I shall cry a little. But only after Betty has gone. Oh!' She put a hand up to her suddenly scarlet cheeks. 'What shall we tell people?'

'More lies,' sighed the marquess. 'We will say that Mr Armitage has taken his grandson to Hopeworth and that we will follow in a few days. Then we will leave for Paris. It will be a very long second honeymoon and the death of our son will be announced while we are away. The few servants that will have to know the truth of the matter will not gossip. Society will quickly forget that we even had a son.'

Betty came in and dropped a curtsy. Charles was lying in a cradle in front of the fire.

'Coming home with Ma, then,' said Betty, scooping him up. One small baby fist went out and clutched very tightly onto the bib of her apron.

Betty bent her head and rested her cheek on the baby's dark hair. She stood very still. Tears ran again from the vicar's eyes and Annabelle turned away to hide her own tears.

'Let us go then, Betty,' said the vicar. 'John is waiting.'

The marquess cleared his throat and tried to lighten the emotion-charged atmosphere.

'Are you going to visit Daphne?'

The vicar shook his head. 'Returning to Hopeworth.'

'Then, good hunting!'

Mr Armitage turned about, his face heavy with

160

remorse and grief.

''Fore George,' he said quietly, 'I'll never hunt again.'

CHAPTER SEVEN

Mr Garfield spent the remainder of the night tossing and turning, images of several different Daphne Armitages flitting through his brain.

He tried to cling to the idea of a vain, frivolous girl who cared for nothing but fashion. Then he would remember Daphne kneeling by the road in an old gown, pleading for his blessing; Daphne pretending to be mad; Daphne cooking that repulsive meal, hugging Bellsire and Thunderer, and defying the guests to harm one hair of their coats. Then there was the Daphne of the Review in Hyde Park, warm and pliant and passionate in his arms, and Daphne of Brighton, lit up from within so that it almost hurt to look at so much beauty.

He got out of bed and bathed his face, wrapped himself in his dressing gown, and sat down at the writing desk. He began to jot down all he knew about Daphne until he came to the subject of the ball he had just attended.

And here was yet another Daphne, glittering like a diamond with something dark and haunted at the back of her eyes.

At last he decided that his hurt pride had caused him to damn her without a trial. Gently bred girls like Daphne did not go around rejecting suitors without one word of explanation.

He decided to call on her after he had had a few

hours' sleep.

But the sun was high in the sky by the time he woke up, a sun that was rapidly disappearing behind an encroaching veil of mist.

By the time he stepped out of doors, the air had that shivery, sooty smell it always carried before London was about to be enveloped in a really sickening, choking sort of fog.

He was very keyed up and nervous by the time he reached Lady Godolphin's house in Hanover Square. What if she would not see him?

His first feeling when Mice told him that the ladies and Mr Archer had gone to the British Museum was one of anti-climax followed by one of disbelief. They could not have gone to the British Museum of all places!

With a glint of humour, Mice volunteered the information that Mr Archer had been much put out, but Miss Daphne had been most insistent that they go. When he arrived at the British Museum he decided to wait in the hall for Daphne and her party to return. They had only just left, having had to wait for another twelve people to make up the tour, since the rule was that fifteen people were to be admitted at one time, neither more nor less. He wondered what Mr Archer thought of it all.

Mr Archer was having a most miserable time and praying that none of the *ton* should see him in such an unfashionable place and with such unfashionable company.

Daphne looked like a dowd. Without the benefit of curl papers or curling tongs, her hair lay flat and smooth, dragged almost painfully back from her forehead and fastened in a bun at the nape of her neck. On top of this hideous hairstyle she wore a depressing kind of felt hat, usually sported by cooks and persons of that order. In fact, Daphne had borrowed it from one of the chambermaids. She wore a drab brown dress, a drab brown cloak, and horror of horrors, half boots. No lady, as Mr Archer knew, had worn half boots for *ages*. Definitely out of fashion.

He felt his misery complete when, on entering the open courtyard of the museum, Daphne took out a pair of small, ugly steel spectacles and popped them on her nose.

After some minutes brooding, Mr Archer became determined to make the best of things. He would stroll among the art treasures, languidly asking a few intelligent questions, thereby showing himself to be one of the virtuosos who knew art and literature as well as they knew the cut of an expensive coat.

Alas, for his dignity. No sooner was the party of fifteen gathered together than the guide appeared, a squat, swarthy German, who set off at an enormous pace, hustling them along, cracking jokes, making lewd *double entendres* as the ladies were breathlessly whipped past nude statues, urging everyone ever forward when any of them showed a disposition to linger.

They charged through rooms full of stuffed animals and birds—many of them seemingly in a state of decay. They were only allowed a glimpse of various arms and costumes—rushed breathlessly around a collection of minerals, then antiquities from Heraklion, Pompeii, and Egypt. The Rosetta stone, several large sarcophagi, numerous statues and bas-reliefs from the French collection which had fallen into the hands of the British in 1801 were admired for the space of about ten seconds and then they were off again at full gallop, into the room full of Mr Towneley's collection of marbles from Greece and Rome. There was a fine statue of Diana, also one of a woman with a startling expression of indignation and terror on her face as if the invading party had just woken her up. Through the manuscripts they hurtled—forty-three volumes of Icelandic literature, presented by Sir Joseph Banks, forty-one volumes of decisions of the commissaries who settled the property boundaries after the great fire of London, a glimpse of the Magna Carta—and then they were back in the hall again with their rude, loud guide holding out his hand for money, which nobody gave him, all being in a breathless state of fury and exhaustion.

If it had not been for the company of Mr Archer and Lady Godolphin, Mr Garfield might not have recognized Daphne.

A slow appreciative smile crossed his face. She looked terrible. She looked dowdy. She looked a mess. She looked adorable.

The elegant Mr Garfield, whose heart had remained for so long untouched, fell head over heels, utterly and completely, right at that moment, with Daphne Armitage. Something finer had been added to the sheer physical desire to possess her. He wanted to cherish her, take care of her, give her his children. He wanted to take her in his arms and kiss away the shadows of worry from her eyes.

He wanted to punch Cyril Archer on the nose.

Daphne did not see him right away since her view of the world was blurred by the spectacles— courtesy of Lady Godolphin's second footman.

It was Lady Godolphin who spotted him.

164

'I'd know those legs anywhere,' she cried enthusiastically. 'Mr Garfield.'

Daphne stood there miserably, her hands going up to take off the hideous glasses.

He *would* find her like this

She had woken up that day with his face in the forefront of her mind. She longed for him. She cursed herself for having lost him. How on earth could she ever have believed her own father capable of . . .

But there was a sort of brutal side to the vicar. A vague memory haunted Daphne of the reverend rolling behind a haystack with a giggling country girl after the harvest had been brought in. There was the time her father had taken his whip, right in the church, to that wicked suitor of Annabelle's. And an innocent mind like Daphne's, half-attracted to, half-afraid of the deep dark secrets of the marriage bed, was quite prepared to believe the worst of anybody. Only look at Lady Godolphin! Age had not dimmed her splendid lechery, nor custom staled her infinite variety of beaux.

Then there was the Countess of Oxford, Jane Elizabeth Harley, that notoriously unfaithful lady. So varied was the paternity of her children that they were called by the wags the 'Harleian Miscellany', the title of a work published by her complaisant husband.

There was Byron, now in exile. The rumour of his affair with his half-sister, Augusta, had reached even Daphne's chaste ears.

And the Prince Regent himself—always falling in love with elderly ladies. Daphne naively believed that only the young and fit had a right to fall in love.

But she still felt miserable and guilty over having believed such a slur on her father's character.

Much of her hopelessness had been relieved by the robust support of Lady Godolphin. There *was* something comforting about a lady who never seemed to be shocked at anything.

But even Lady Godolphin could not help her now.

Daphne knew she looked terrible. She had thrown all her armour away. She was not clever or bright or sophisticated. She was quite sure her only attraction for Mr Garfield had lain in her beauty.

Lady Godolphin cheerfully urged Mr Garfield to return with them to Hanover Square—'for if you was wantin' to see the museum, don't. Not that there mightn't be something interesting, except that Grimaldi of a guide won't let anybody stop for breath.'

Daphne stood with her head turned away, conscious of the possessive presence of Mr Archer standing very close beside her.

Mr Archer was wary of Mr Garfield. His normally dim intelligence sharpened by jealousy, he felt sure Mr Garfield had only come to the museum to see Daphne. Daphne looked remarkably Friday-faced so perhaps it was as well he should see her thus. But, thought Mr Archer viciously, Daphne is not going to shame me by looking like a frump. If needs be, I will threaten her again.

A rather nasty look crossed his beautiful features causing Mr Garfield to think that Archer was like some paintings. Much better when seen from a distance.

Short of telling Mr Archer to go and Mr Garfield to stay, Lady Godolphin did not know how to resolve the situation. She noticed the amused glint in Mr Garfield's eyes as he watched Daphne and also noticed the way Daphne's colour came and went.

When they were all settled in the drawing room at Lady Godolphin's, Mr Garfield, very much at his ease, chatted of Brighton, and this and that. Daphne asked shyly about Mr Apsley, although privately she did not care one rap for that callous young man's welfare, and Mr Garfield smiled and said Mr Apsley was in love again and therefore restored to his normal, cheerful, non-interfering self.

Mr Archer looked sulky.

Mr Garfield apologized for his prolonged absence from the polite world but explained he had been much engaged with his business. Mr Garfield was urged to describe his business to the ladies.

Mr Archer yawned rudely.

Lady Godolphin marvelled that such a man as Mr Garfield who came from an aristocratic family with so much money should engage in trade.

'I was one of the first troops to go out with Wellington to the Peninsula,' said Mr Garfield. Daphne thought of him in uniform and her mouth went dry.

The fog had thickened outside and the candles were lit, a branch of them on the mantel above Mr Garfield's head sparking copper glints in his thick hair.

'I was wounded,' went on Mr Garfield, 'and did not see very much action. I was still very young when I was invalided home. I gambled a great deal and seemed, well on my way to losing my family's fortune. My mother was dead and my father, ailing.

Then a friend of mine lost heavily at the tables and shot himself through the mouth—I beg your pardon, Miss Daphne. It shocked me so much. My life suddenly seemed useless. Then another gambling friend, a man much older than I, met me one day in Bond Street and told me he had entered the world of trade and had managed to restore his fortune. I was fascinated by his tale and went with him to the City where I fell immediately in love with the world of trade and commerce. It was a milieu in which I could gamble in a way and yet reap the benefits of hard work, long hours, and an unexpected gift for business. Perhaps my connection with trade may give you a disgust of me, Miss Daphne.'

Daphne shook her head.

'I call it a betrayal of our class,' said Mr Archer with rare animation. 'Don't you feel you smell of the shop?'

'Don't you feel you are being rude enough to warrant me calling you out?' countered Mr Garfield with a sweet smile.

Mr Archer relapsed into resentful muttering. He *had* to talk to Daphne. He had to be sure of her. But the fog was thickening rapidly outside and his hand strayed nervously to the white glory of his cravat, already imagining the gentle rain of soot that must already be falling outside.

Lady Godolphin, becoming weary and remembering her own love troubles, at last sighed and looked pointedly at the clock. She had also decided that the whole mess about Annabelle's baby could simply be decided by asking Annabelle. She planned to send Daphne upstairs to lie down and rest before the rigours of the evening. They

168

were all to go and see Kemble in *Lear*. Shakespeare was a playwright Lady Godolphin considered infinitely boring and she hoped the sight and sound of the mad king prosing on for quite three hours would agonize Mr Archer just as much as she was sure it would agonize herself.

The gentlemen rose, Lady Godolphin rang the bell, and they were shown out.

After Daphne had trailed upstairs, Lady Godolphin sat and thought about Colonel Arthur Brian. The more she thought, the more miserable she became. It was all so hopeless. She would never see him again.

Her thoughts were so gloomy, so unutterably hopeless, so despairing, that she was almost beginning to enjoy herself when Mice announced the return of Mr Garfield.

Lady Godolphin brightened slightly as she always brightened at the sight of a handsome man.

'Forgot something, Mr Garfield?' she asked. 'Forgive me for not rising. I have the vapours.'

Mr Garfield eyed the plump figure of Lady Godolphin, which was stretched out on the sofa, with sympathetic amusement.

'I will only take up a little of your time, my lady. What is the matter with Miss Daphne? Something is troubling her badly.'

'Oh, pooh!' sighed Lady Godolphin. 'What a Cheltenham tragedy has been enacted. But it is all well now, or will be as soon as I speak to that totty-headed sister of hers.'

'I do not think Miss Daphne indifferent to me,' said Mr Garfield, taking a turn about the room. Lady Godolphin watched the play of muscles on his thighs and sighed gustily. 'I told her at Brighton

169

that I wished to marry her and she accepted. I did not ask her in so many words but I told her I would call on her father the following day. The next thing I knew she had quitted Brighton without even leaving a note, and, furthermore, that she had subsequently become engaged to Archer.'

'I thought she had told me everything,' complained Lady Godolphin. 'As if thinking her pa had committed incest with Annabelle were not . . .'

'My lady!'

'Oh, lor'!' Lady Godolphin looked guiltily at Mr Garfield. 'It's all a farradiddle. Archer overheard Mr Armitage saying as how he had been able to give Annabelle a baby when her husband could not. So he thought the worst. So he tells Daphne he'll spread the whole story about London if she don't marry him.'

'How on earth could anyone believe such a thing?'

'Seen the baby?' demanded Lady Godolphin. 'Got a look o' Charles as he is now. Can't blame Daphne. Frightened out of her wits. Baby ain't Annabelle's, mark you. But stands to reason it can't be Mr Armitage's, not but what it might be one of his by-blows, if you take my meaning, but not by his own flesh and blood.'

'And what did Mr Armitage and Lady Brabington have to say when you confronted them with this monstrous accusation?'

'I haven't had the time,' said Lady Godolphin crossly. 'I shall write to Charles, summoning him to London. Daphne only told me after the ball. I decided to try to give Archer a disgust of her in the meantime by takin' him to the British Museum and letting Daphne get herself up like a fright. I had

170

just decided to call on Annabelle but I was taken with the vapours, my heart being broke.'

'Colonel Arthur Brian,' announced Mice lugubriously.

Lady Godolphin twisted her head on the sofa cushion and gazed incredulously at the spare figure of the colonel who was framed in the doorway, leaning on his cane.

'My love,' he said brokenly. 'I could not rest until I saw you. There has been no other woman who has touched my soul like you.'

Mr Garfield opened his mouth to demand further information about the mess his beloved appeared to have become embroiled in, but Lady Godolphin held out her fat arms, Colonel Arthur Brian threw away his cane, darted across the room and fell on top of her.

It looked, thought Mr Garfield, eyeing the thin elderly back sourly, as if the colonel had fallen face down on a feather bed.

He went out and quietly closed the door behind him.

He stood in the hall, irresolute. Should he send for Daphne?

He decided he wanted to slay this particular dragon for her and lay it at her feet before he spoke to her again. How amazingly stupid to go through all this agony and not just ask where the wretched baby came from.

Automatically adjusting his curly-brimmed beaver to the correct angle, he made his way out into the fog.

Daphne was not asleep. She was worrying over the disappearance of the maid, Betty. Lady Godolphin must be informed and the authorities alerted. Daphne had questioned the servants and was appalled to find out that Betty had been missing for days. She had assumed the sulky maid had simply been keeping away from her and not performing her duties as lady's maid out of some strange feeling of pique.

Daphne made her way downstairs. The house was silent. Lady Godolphin had not been in her bedchamber.

She pushed open the door of the drawing room.

The sight that met her eyes scandalized her so much that for what seemed an age but was in fact only a few seconds she could only stand and stare.

Then she whipped herself out of the room, her heart beating painfully and her breathing constricted.

Who could she turn to now that her one support was gone? Now that her one support was playing some peculiar kind of naked leapfrog with Colonel Arthur Brian.

Hopeworth was very far away.

Minerva!

Minerva was the one she should have turned to. Now that she no longer believed her father capable of such a heinous sin, Daphne longed for Minerva's quiet voice and cool touch.

She returned to her room and changed into more fashionable clothes: a merino gown with a thick grey cloak lined with damask to cover it, York tan gloves on her hands, and a modish bonnet on her head.

She rang for Mice and ordered the carriage to be brought round and then went downstairs, making as much noise as possible, frightened that the doors of the drawing room would fly open to reveal that terrible sight again.

Although Minerva lived only a short way away the fog was so thick that the carriage had to edge slowly through it while two footmen walked ahead, bearing flaming torches to light the way.

By the time they reached Minerva's home Daphne was frozen to the bone, despite the thick fur carriage rugs over her knees and the hot brick at her feet.

She felt if Minerva proved to be absent, then she simply could not bear it.

But Minerva was there, her eyes lighting up with concern as they fell on Daphne's white, strained face.

She drew her into the downstairs saloon, calling to the servants to bring a glass of negus and to build up the fire. Daphne huddled in a chair, her teeth chattering, while Minerva knelt before her and rubbed at her hands to get them warm.

Minerva was feeling very worried and guilty. Something terrible had obviously happened, and the sight of the pinched and shivering Daphne brought back memories of the young Daphne, as she had been before she became obsessed with her own beauty.

'Now what is the matter?' asked Minerva gently. 'There is nothing so bad that we cannot put it right. Sylvester is at his club. Would you like me to send for him?'

Daphne shook her head and a large tear rolled down her cheek.

Minerva stood up and untied the strings of Daphne's bonnet and smoothed her hair back from her brow with a gentle hand.

'You must tell me what ails you, Daphne. Else

how can I help?'

Daphne gulped and sobbed and the whole story came pouring out. In all her distress, Daphne could not help noticing with a sort of wonder that Minerva did not look in the slightest shocked.

Minerva was, in fact, too busy chastising herself for having neglected Daphne's welfare so badly; for having judged her own sister so harshly on mere surface appearance.

Minerva was forcibly reminded of the horrors of her own visit to London. The idea of their father having committed incest was so ludicrous it was the only thing that made her want to smile. She would well understand how a girl as innocent and naive as Daphne, exposed to all the whispers and gossip of society, could believe such a tale, and also understand her frantic determination to try to protect her family by herself.

'But what is Lady Godolphin about?' demanded Minerva at last. 'Has she not done something? Did she not think to ask Annabelle where the baby came from? All poor Papa said was, "You know," which means he agrees the baby is not Annabelle's, but that was all. I think you are all quite, quite mad.'

'Lady Godolphin,' said Daphne, blushing to the roots of her hair, 'has just become reconciled with Colonel Brian and is too occupied at the moment to . . .'

'Oh, how shamefully I have behaved!' cried Minerva. 'To leave you in the care of that so very kind but so very shocking lady. But you did really fool us all, Daphne dear. Do you remember when you left Brighton? I was quite cross with you for encouraging poor Mr Garfield and then leaving, and all you would say coldly was that Brighton bored you and we were not modish enough! When I heard you had become engaged to Mr Archer, I was still angry with you and thought you *deserved* each other. Your brothers-in-law were not consulted because Brabington was away at the time as well as Desire, and Sylvester would only laugh and say he would not believe the pair of you would ever reach the altar, and it was just as well to let you "get it out of your system". Drink your negus and we will go immediately to Annabelle, and then we will let the gentlemen deal with Mr Archer!'

*   *   *

Mr Garfield was finding his visit to the Brabingtons much harder than he had anticipated. He was seated with the Marquess of Brabington, discussing an excellent bottle of port. Annabelle was dressing and would join them shortly. Everything seemed so quiet and normal. How on earth could he broach the subject? 'Well, Brabington, and how's your little bastard coming along?'

He was just about to make a start somehow when the door opened and Annabelle tripped into the room.

She was much changed from the last time he had seen her. Gone was the petulant spoiled beauty, and in her place a mature and glowing woman with eyes only for her husband.

Their happiness was almost tangible. The marquess refilled Mr Garfield's glass, leaned back in his chair, and asked, 'And to what do we owe the pleasure of this visit, Garfield?'

Mr Garfield searched wildly for any polite and

175

social opening and could think of none.

He simply plunged in and told the story of the blackmailing of Daphne in as curt and brief a manner as possible.

Mr Garfield had a strong desire to slap Lady Brabington, who succumbed to a helpless fit of the giggles, choking over and over again, 'Papa! And I? How rich! How exquisite! I always said Daphne had more hair than wit.'

'You are behaving badly, my love,' said the Marquess of Brabington coldly, and Annabelle hurriedly apologized. 'Do not be cross with me, Peter,' she said. 'You know I always giggle when things really upset me. That is when I am at my most silliest. You must forgive me, Mr Garfield, as well. Papa came this very day and took the baby away. Oh, Peter will explain everything.'

And explain he did, while Mr Garfield was torn between relief, amusement, and anger against the Reverend Charles Armitage who he damned as an unfeeling, stupid parent.

'So what will we do now?' asked Annabelle when all the explanations were over.

'I think Mr Garfield is perfectly capable of silencing Mr Archer,' said the marquess, 'or would you like some help, Garfield?'

'No,' said that gentleman grimly, 'I am quite capable of silencing him myself.'

Annabelle gave a little shriek. 'You will not kill him?'

'Not I,' said Mr Garfield, striding to the door. 'He is not worth going to the scaffold for.'

*   *   *

Mr Archer was sitting in Watier's, gloomily playing at hazard. He had already thrown 'crabs' twice, and his partner had just thrown a main and 'nicked it', meaning he had won all the stakes. Mr Archer only played hazard because it was fashionable. He did not like losing money which should otherwise be spent on clothes.

He had called at Lady Godolphin's to escort Daphne to the theatre and had been told coldly by the butler that Miss Daphne was not at home and her ladyship was not receiving guests. He had taken himself off to the play and wandered moodily up and down until he was sure Daphne was nowhere to be seen.

He wished heartily he had never looked in at Watier's. He began to wish it even more when, feeling himself observed, he looked straight up into the glaring yellow eyes of Mr Simon Garfield.

Mr Garfield leaned across the table, picked up Mr Archer's glass of wine and threw it full in his face.

'What did you do that for?' screamed Mr Archer, mopping his face.

'I do not like your waistcoat, sir,' said Mr Garfield. 'It is an offence to the polite eye.'

The players around the table sat motionless. There was something so terrifying about Mr Garfield's cold rage that not one man wanted to draw attention to himself. And Mr Archer had no friends.

Mr Garfield walked around the table, took Mr Archer's coat by the collar and roughly jerked him to his fcct. 'I should have known a *lady* like you would not dare to call me out,' he jeered.

Mr Archer sweated. The last thing he wanted

to do was challenge anyone to a duel, particularly Mr Simon Garfield.

'You are drunk!' he squeaked.

'Then let us find some cool night air. Will you come with me quietly or do I have to carry you out?'

With an almost feminine scream, Mr Archer clutched at the table, his long nails digging into the green baize. 'Help!' he screamed.

The club servants came running.

Mr Garfield gave them an icy look, drew back his fist and slammed it into Mr Archer's chin. Mr Archer slumped over the table.

'Drunk again,' said Mr Garfield, shaking his head. 'I shall just have to take him home.'

He glared about the room. 'No one, I trust,' he said silkily, 'is going to stop me from taking my *friend*, Mr Archer, home.'

The players cleared their throats, once more the, dice box rattled, the servants drew back.

Mr Garfield stooped and slung Mr Archer over his shoulder and strode from the club.

Mr Archer slowly regained consciousness. His first thought on seeing the familiar surroundings of his lodgings was one of intense relief. Then he realized he was not alone. He was lying on his own sofa and Mr Garfield was glaring down at him.

'Don't kill me,' bleated Mr Archer, trying to rise.

'I am not going to kill you, much as I would like to,' said Mr Garfield. 'You, my friend, are going on a long journey. You are going to make the Grand Tour. *You* threaten Miss Daphne with scandal. You! What if London should know of that hyacinth you had in keeping some years ago? You have been guilty of a crime punishable by death. I could turn you over to the authorities.'

'You *can't* know. He died of the fever. There's no proof.' Mr Archer was white to the lips.

'No, but there is the weapon of gossip and I will not hesitate to use it against you if you are still in London in the next two hours. I have told your servants you are leaving. Your trunks are packed.'

'I will go. I will go. Don't hit me again,' babbled Mr Archer.

'Very well. Tell me, Archer, why did a creature such as you wish to marry?'

Mr Archer hung his head. A large tear plopped onto the wooden boards at his feet.

Mr Garfield was seized with an awful pity. 'Just be sure you are not here tomorrow,' he said quietly. 'There is no foundation for the scurrilous tale about Mr Armitage you threatened to put about, so you have no weapons left.'

He turned on his heel and walked out of the room and down the stairs.

Out in the street, he was met by a solid wall of greyish-black fog.

Holding a handkerchief up to his mouth, Mr Garfield picked his way carefully along the street, while upstairs in the room above Mr Archer sat and shivered, holding his body tightly in his arms, and listening to the footsteps dying away in the night.

CHAPTER EIGHT

Mr Simon Garfield wandered on through the fog until he found himself turning in at Hanover Square. It was past midnight but carriages still crawled through the fog. He rapped loudly at the door, and waited. He had to see Daphne and tell her that all was well.

After some time, he heard the sound of bolts being drawn back and Mice's large white moon of a face peered cautiously around the door.

'Oh, Mr Garfield, sir,' he said. 'The ladies are abed. Miss Daphne arrived home not a half hour before in the company of Lord and Lady Sylvester. Lady Sylvester saw her put to bed and then left.'

Mr Garfield fished in his pocket and drew out a gold coin. 'Do you think, Mice,' he said, 'that you could ask Miss Daphne to step downstairs?'

Mice looked doubtfully at the money. A guinea now might mean no job on the morrow. On the other hand, Lady Godolphin was not likely to stir out of bed, not now she had company in it.

'Very well, sir,' he said, cautiously pocketing the money.

Mr Garfield was led into the Green Saloon. Mice busied himself lighting the fire and then left.

The clocks ticked sonorously. The fire crackled in the hearth. Mr Garfield began to think she would not come.

And then the doors were opened and Daphne entered the room and smiled at him shyly.

'I came to tell you, Miss Daphne,' said Mr Garfield, feeling stiff and pompous, that I have constrained Mr Archer to flee the country. He will not trouble you again.'

'Thank you,' said Daphne. 'Oh, thank you so much. Lord Brabington assured me you would deal with the matter.'

'You have seen him? Ah, then you know the mystery of the baby. I can find it in my heart to

180

be sorry for your father. Why is it such a beautiful innocent as yourself could believe something so vile?'

'So many vile things happen,' said Daphne, blushing, 'and everyone in London society whispers about them and pretends to be shocked although they are not in the least. There are so many things I do not understand. All is rigid propriety and manners on the surface, and underneath . . .' She gave a shudder.

He turned away a little and Daphne studied him anxiously. Had he *only* come to tell her about Mr Archer? He looked so handsome with his thick copper hair gleaming in the light and his heavy-lidded eyes surveying her so strangely.

'We have had a very informal introduction to each other, Miss Daphne,' he said at last. 'I confess I have not behaved very well towards you . . . not in the way I should have *liked* to behave.'

So he had not wanted to kiss her. Overwrought and tired, Daphne began to feel angry.

'I am not in the way,' he went on, 'of mauling gently bred ladies in Hyde Park nor for that matter do I often kiss strange country wenches by the roadside.'

'It is very late,' said Daphne crossly. 'I am exceeding grateful to you for having rid me of Mr Archer and I would like to stand here and listen to a catalogue of your virtues all night, but I confess I am monstrous tired.'

He looked at her with irritation. 'Miss Daphne, I was about to explain my honourable intentions of courting you at length so that we might get to know each other better. My thoughts of you are of the purest.'

For one brief moment, it seemed as if Annabelle had taken over Daphne, as she tossed her head and replied without a blush, 'How very disappointing.'

He made an exasperated noise and walked up to her and pulled her roughly into his arms and kissed her breathless.

'You are a shameless baggage,' he said at last, giving her a little shake. 'If you say such bold things to me, you are not to be 'trusted. I always thought you should have a keeper. You are going to marry me soon.'

'Yes, Simon,' said Daphne Armitage demurely. 'Kiss me again.'

He smiled down at her, and this time drew her very gently against him and slowly bent his lips to hers, brushing her mouth softly with his own, then deepening the caress as he felt her begin to quiver in his arms.

She seemed to turn to fire and flame and he lifted her into his arms, carried her to a chair by the fire where he set her on his knees, and then began to make love to every part of her that he could decently reach.

His senses soared and rocketed, the chair creaked and protested under their frenzied writhings, and just as Mr Garfield had boldly moved from the decent to the indecent, just as his mouth was lovingly beginning to trace the contours of one bared breast, a screech like an apoplectic parrot stopped him dead.

Lady Godolphin stood in the doorway, a candle in one hand

'Upstairs to your bed, miss,' she said sternly to Daphne, 'and I will have a word with you later. To think a gently reared girl like yourself should allow any gentleman to see her in such des-habillies. Go!'

Daphne straightened her gown and looked shyly up at Mr Garfield.

He took her hand in a firm clasp. 'We are to be married, Lady Godolphin.'

'Oh.' A smile of pleasure and relief spread across Lady Godolphin's features. 'Nonetheless,' she said, 'you'll have to leave carryings-on like that until after the wedding. I was never more shocked.'

'How is Colonel Brian?' asked Daphne sweetly. 'Oh, ah,' said Lady Godolphin, turning pink. 'He has decided to stay with us for a little.'

'I shall go to Hopeworth tomorrow,' said Mr Garfield, 'and obtain Mr Armitage's permission to pay my addresses to Daphne.'

'We'll all go,' said Lady Godolphin. Better to get Arthur away from the fleshpots and temptations of London, she thought. He wouldn't find anything else to do in Hopeworth except pay attention to herself.

*　　　*　　　*

Squire Radford stood in the shelter of the hedge at the bottom of the garden and watched the squat figure of the vicar going about his parish rounds.

His horses and hounds were to be put up for sale at Hopeminster the following week.

The vicar had not resigned his living. He had not gone to see the bishop. Instead he had returned to Hopeworth, set Betty, her husband and baby up in style in a trim cottage, and then proceeded to try to turn himself into a saint.

From matins to evensong, the church was open seven days a week. The parishioners were visited

183

by their vicar as they had never been visited before. The poor of the parish were taken care of as they had never been taken care of before. The vicar counselled, advised, helped and preached.

He was more unpopular than he had ever been in his life before.

His congregation quailed before his ranting sermons. They were tired of being harangued into atoning for their sins.

Villagers hid behind their furniture and pretended to be out when they saw his shovel hat bobbing past their cottage windows. Mothers began to threaten their children with, 'If you ain't good, the Reverend Armitage'll come and get you.'

Squire Radford sighed. Charles was dismal company. There were no more friendly suppers and sharing a bottle beside the library fire. The vicar no longer drank anything stronger than lemonade. He was even running an anti-tea campaign.

The Squire noticed the vicar was on his way to the Hall to pay a visit to his brother, Sir Edwin Armitage. Well, it couldn't happen to a better fellow.

Sir Edwin quailed when he heard his brother had come visiting. Lady Armitage promptly declared she had the headache and Josephine and Emily refused to accompany him downstairs. Josephine had at last become affianced to a middle-aged squire over in Hopeminster and Sir Edwin was only too glad to have one of his daughters finally engaged. He blamed the Armitage girls at the vicarage for having enticed away all the best beaux, forgetting that they had found their husbands in London and not in the neighbourhood. It was only a small consolation to him that Daphne was

184

marrying someone very ordinary in the person of Mr Archer.

Sir Edwin minced into the drawing room and looked nervously at the squat figure of his brother. Sir Edwin was dressed as usual in the height of fashion, his clothes more suited to a Bond Street lounger than to a middle-aged country baronet.

The vicar greeted him with, ' "For we wrestle not against flesh and blood, but against the principalities, against powers, against the rulers of the darkness of the world, against spiritual wickedness in high places." '

Sir Edwin polished his quizzing glass on his sleeve and then surveyed his brother. 'You sound like a demned radical,' he said.

Undeterred, the vicar ploughed on. ' "To obey is better than sacrifice",' he said conversationally, 'and to hearken than the fat of rams . . ." '

'What the dooce are you on about?' demanded Sir Edwin crossly. 'Been at the communion wine?'

'No, I have not,' said the vicar wrathfully. 'I shun all liquor. I abominate tea.'

'Splendid,' said Sir Edwin maliciously, 'for I have just received a pipe of very rare port from town and was going to offer you some, but now I don't need to.'

The vicar's left eyelid twitched.

'Got Josephine pushed off onto a squire, then,' he remarked with somewhat of his old manner.

'Ah, yes, a most estimable man. The sale of your pack and your horses has caused great excitement in the county, Charles. I wonder you bear to part with them. Do you not feel you are taking all this religion rather seriously?'

'It's my job to take it seriously,' snapped the

vicar. 'I'm a man o' God.'

'And to what do we owe the pleasure of this second coming?' demanded Sir Edwin.

'Your daughters have not been to confession.'

'Oh, tut! Tut! Really, Charles, you go too far. They will go to confession if they wish. We have all been doing very nicely under the gentle and undemanding care of Mr Pettifor, your curate. We are not used in Hopeworth to having to suffer under the tongue lash of a Methodist.'

'I ain't no Methody,' howled the vicar, 'and if I weren't such a good man, I'd call you out for that.'

'Oh, call yourself out of my house,' said his brother wearily, 'and come back when your fevered brain has cooled down.'

The vicar stomped out of the Hall and made his way home. He intended to spend the rest of the afternoon studying his Bible. Soon he was cosily ensconced in his study, reading St Mark, scowling horribly and moving his lips as he followed the words, 'For from within out of the heart of man, proceed evil thoughts, adulteries, fornications, murders, an evil eye, blasphemy, pride, foolishness. All these things come from within and defile the man.'

'True. Terribly true,' muttered the vicar with gloomy satisfaction.

His study door crashed open and his daughter Diana stood on the threshold. Her wild mane of hair was windblown and her eyes large, sparkling and defiant in her thin, high-cheekboned face.

'Has Daphne said anything to you?' she demanded.

'No, my love,' said the vicar sweetly.

'Then there's no hope,' said Diana, wearily

slumping down into a battered leather armchair on the other side of the desk. 'Funny, Daphne was always the meek one and yet I thought she'd somehow make you change your mind.'

'About what?'

'About me going hunting.'

'Alas, my poor child. I have brought you up in sin and wickedness. I am to sell that terrible indulgence of mine.'

'Stop this rubbish!' screamed Diana. 'Stop it, I say. Do you know what cant you are talking? Do you know what you are doing? You are selling off piecemeal one of the best packs in England. You are terrifying the parishioners with your ranting ways. You are driving people away from the church.'

She lowered her voice and leaned one elbow on the desk, fixing her father with bright, wild eyes. 'Listen, Father. One day you let me go with you a little way, up on the rise above Hopeworth. Do you remember? It was two years ago. We trotted up that deep-rutted lane with the day breaking from purple to gold; we looked down on the farms and the mist-coiled river. Do you remember the golden beech woods in the early sunshine, all those drifts of yellow leaves falling about the mossy roots? And the excitement! The tension building up. Do you remember John Summer's cry, "Gone away"?'

'Stop!' said the vicar, putting his hands over his ears.

'No, I will not stop,' said Diana. She stood up and leaned over her father as he sat with his head bowed. 'I suggest you go straight to church now and ask the good Lord to take your addled brains out and tuck them back the right way again.'

She slammed out, crashing the door behind her with such force that the whole vicarage rocked.

The Reverend Armitage sat there for a long time. Then he put on his hat and wearily went out and along to the church. He entered by the side door and sat down in one of the pews, enjoying the novelty of looking up at the pulpit instead of looking down from it.

Mr Garfield's expert was doing very well. Now gold leaf glinted on the wings of the cherubim up on the roof, and already the worm-eaten pews at the back had been replaced with new oak ones.

He bent his head in prayer. It was a muddled half-formed prayer for guidance. Before he had prayed on his knees, ferociously and earnestly promising to atone for his sins. Now he asked for help in a friendly way, rather as if he were talking to Squire Radford.

At last he rose and went out into the peace of the early evening. All at once he felt very normal and ordinary. He could not quite explain it, but he felt neither very good nor very bad.

He took a deep breath of fresh air. It smelled of evergreen and woodsmoke and damp, rotting leaves.

Squire Radford heard someone whistling *Brighton Beach* and twitched the curtain and looked out of his library window. The Reverend Charles Armitage, whistling jauntily, was strolling up the drive.

The squire let out a long sigh of relief. 'Ram,' he said over his shoulder, 'the very *best* port, I think, and set two places for dinner.'

* * *

The vicar strolled homewards after an excellent dinner, well content with the world. It was pleasant to feel comfortable inside his own skin again.

A blustery, jolly wind was tossing the bare branches and a hunter's moon rode high above.

The sight of two carriages drawn up outside the vicarage door made him pause, his pleasure momentarily dimmed by the thought that the bishop might have come to call.

Then he espied Lady Godolphin's lozenge on one of the panels.

Whistling cheerfully, he walked into the vicarage parlour.

The whistle died on his lips.

Daphne, Mr Garfield, Lady Godolphin, Colonel Arthur Brian, Diana, Frederica, and his wife were all lined up, obviously waiting for him. He thought uneasily that they looked like a jury deliberating on a particularly nasty murder.

'Hey, ho!' said the vicar. 'What's to do?'

Daphne rose to her feet. 'I must have a word with you in private.'

'Oh. About something you've all cooked up between you by the look of it,' growled the vicar. 'Very well, miss. You may follow me.'

He led the way into the study and closed the door behind them.

'Now, miss,' he said. 'I don't suppose I may hope for good news? That's Garfield in there.'

'You may ask for good news on one condition,' said Daphne primly.

'Which is?'

'I will marry Mr Garfield if you keep your hunt . . .'

189

'Done! Already decided on that.'

'*And* if you allow Diana to go hunting.'

'Now look, Daphne,' said the vicar, 'it does you credit. Thought you wanted to marry Archer?'

Daphne looked at her father in amazement and then realized he did not know the story of Mr Archer's coercion. She could only hope he never did. For if he did he would demand to know what had prompted Archer to think he had a hold over her.

'No. I do not want to marry Mr Archer. I will marry Mr Garfield. But only if you allow Diana to hunt.'

The vicar thought of the Garfield fortune, he thought of the triumph of having another successful marriage in the family, he thought of Diana hunting with him and frowned. But he could deal with that in the future. He might find a way around it.

'Very well then,' he said.

Daphne pulled forward the copy of the Bible that the vicar had been reading earlier.

'Swear on the Bible, Papa.'

'Not even trusted by my own daughter,' grumbled the vicar. But nonetheless, he pulled forward the Bible and said, 'I solemnly do swear that Diana may go hunting with me.'

'Oh, Papa,' laughed Daphne. 'Now I have tricked you, for I would have married Mr Garfield whatever you said.'

'Minx,' said the vicar. But he could not help grinning at her happiness.

They went back to the parlour, arm in arm. Daphne shouted the good news and everyone cheered, even Mrs Armitage, although she did not quite know what she was cheering about.

'Glad to see you in your right mind, Charles,' said Lady Godolphin. 'We was told you'd gone all rantin' and ravin' and striking fear into the hearts of everyone.'

Had he? To the vicar it all seemed like a bad dream.

Daphne and Mr Garfield were standing over by the window, gazing into each other's eyes, and the vicar heaved a sentimental sigh of satisfaction.

'When can we go hunting, Papa?' came Diana's voice at his elbow.

'Hey, what! Well, as to that, Diana,' said the vicar with a furtive look round to make sure no one was listening. 'There's one little bit of a condition.'

'Which is?'

The vicar mopped his brow. 'I would like you to wear an old coat and breeches o' the twins when you come out with me,' he said. 'And tuck that hair o' yourn under a hat. Don't want no one to know there's a female with the hunt. Wouldn't do, you see.'

'Oh, is *that* all,' laughed Diana. 'I will gladly wear boy's clothes. I do not want to be a girl anyway and I am never going to marry.'

Daphne caught the last part of this exchange. 'Diana, I know that you will fall in love one day and be as happy as I.'

'Pooh!' said Diana Armitage as she thrust her hands in the pockets of her riding dress. 'Never!'

Daphne turned back to her fiance. 'Do you really love me?' she asked anxiously.

'Now, haven't I told you enough?' smiled Mr Garfield.

Lady Godolphin's voice was raised in the corner.
'Arthur,' she was saying, 'I feel I should urge

191

Diana to be careful and always ride sidesaddle. Young Miss Betts, her that was so pretty, well she *would* ride astride just like a man and she went and broke her hymnal before the wedding day and her husband kept screaming she was Haymarket ware.'

'Let us go into the garden, my love,' whispered Mr Garfield. 'For I fear if we stay near Lady Godolphin much longer then the purity of our minds will be well and truly corrupted!'

CHIVERS
LARGE
PRINT
-direct-

If you have enjoyed this Large Print book
and would like to build up your own
collection of Large Print books, please
contact

Chivers Large Print Direct

Chivers Large Print Direct offers you
a full service:

• Prompt mail order service

• Easy-to-read type

• The very best authors

• Special low prices

For further details either call
Customer Services on (01225) 336552
or write to us at Chivers Large Print Direct,
FREEPOST, Bath BA1 3ZZ

Telephone Orders:
FREEPHONE 08081 72 74 75